NIGHTMARE IN COPENHAGEN

by Martha Albrand

Whitney Parker, a young American scientist, suspected that some sinister meaning lay hidden behind the urgent cable that summoned him to Denmark. But he was hardly prepared, on his arrival, for the newspaper head-line that announced the death of his wartime friend, Anders Ørsted.

Knowing that Anders had once worked on explosives, Whitney guessed that the cryptic message had some momentous connection with a new scientific discovery. As he probed further, he found his search for clues gradually reaching out into Sweden and the Russian Zone of Germany.

Though unable at first to find even a trace of the secret explosive, Whitney suddenly found himself in a des-perate dilemma—with the choice of possibly causing the death of thousands of innocent victims or causing the death of his closest friend.

In this taut, thrill-packed story of international intrigue, there are entwined a touching love story, conflicting loyalties, machinations of patriotism and terror, and the stark predicament of a man who holds in his hands the power of life and death over other human beings.

NIGHTMARE IN COPENHAGEN

Martha Albrand

Nightmare in Copenhagen

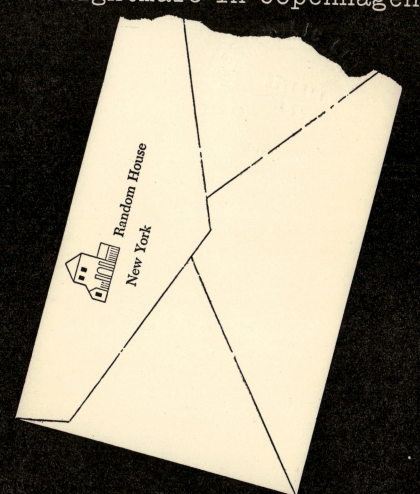

Random House
New York

All the persons and events in this book are entirely imaginary. Nothing in it derives from anything that ever happened.

NIGHTMARE IN COPENHAGEN

Petersen, one of the passport control officers at Kastrup, Copenhagen's airport, was a little old man, due to be retired in two months. He could not get used to the idea. Miserably he stared through the window, out onto the field. Quite a few of the heavy concrete blocks the Germans had placed as obstacles on the runways were still there. But new aprons had been built and now the blocks which had not been removed were used as markers.

Whenever Petersen thought of the terrible years of the Occupation, his throat contracted with pride. Silently, determinedly, without arms, without any outside help to speak of, the Danes had resisted. They had fought the Germans, and Petersen, among thousands of other patriots, had done his share, working underground and risking his life. And somehow, like millions all over the world, when it was over, he had thought there could never be another war.

Perhaps it wasn't so bad, after all, to be old. Then he

saw the DC-6, a streak of silver as the sun caught it, and all he could think of was that in a little while he would no longer be here to watch the planes land, would no longer be part of the excitement and adventure of travel.

By the time he had returned to his desk and got out his stamps and papers and lists, the tourists were streaming into the building. The first in line was a tall young man. American, thought Petersen, even before he had seen the greenish color of his passport. You could always tell by the way they behaved, as if the world were theirs without barriers; at least there was no barrier that could be put up by a minor official in a foreign country.

"I trust you had a good flight, sir. Ever been in Denmark before?"

"Never," said Whitney Parker, and he smiled a little because it seemed incongruous that none of the plans for a visit Ørsted and he had made years ago should have come true before. Somehow work, or perhaps just life, had always made this trip impossible. And without the cable, so guardedly phrased that its text could mean nothing to anybody who didn't know that the interests of the United States might be involved, he wouldn't be here now.

"The purpose of your visit?"

"To see the country. Just put down tourist."

4

Petersen was enjoying the whole rigmarole of red tape. He asked another question. "What will your address be during your stay here?"

There seemed no reason why Whitney shouldn't tell the truth, why he shouldn't say, "Care of Anders Ørsted." But suddenly he remembered the moment when he had torn open the cable, the feeling of alarm with which he had read it again and again—"In mutual interest come as soon as possible"—and now as then he experienced a sense of secrecy and excitement.

He shrugged. "I'll be moving about, I guess, to see as much as I can."

Petersen, though, had noticed the second of hesitation before Whitney answered. He glanced away from the seal and signature of the American State Department and, with a look that took in the whole appearance of Whitney C. Parker as well as the opposite page headed, "Description of bearer," read, "Height: six feet one inch. Hair: brown. Eyes: brown." Under "Distinguishing marks or features" were three lines each canceled with three "x's."

Now that's funny, thought Petersen, and gave the young man standing in front of him another good look. I could have sworn there would be some remark. Yet his searching eyes could discover nothing that would justify a detailed description. Perhaps the forehead was unusually wide and high, perhaps the eyes, their inward look contrasting strongly with the full, smiling mouth, gave the impression that there was something special about the shape and lines of this face. But there was no scar, no disfiguration, no dissimilarity in the color of eyes or skin, no missing finger, no limp to the walk.

Petersen read on: "Date of birth: May 10, 1923." He felt tempted once more to indulge in his own reflections. The young man, smiling at him as though he didn't mind the tedious chore of going through passport control and customs, looked at the same time younger and older than thirty years. There was something boyish about the way he carried himself, something as carefree and uninhibited as a child that still believes he can catch a falling star and carry away in his hands a wonderful new world. But when he stopped smiling, as he did now, he looked suddenly wise and weary like a man who has few illusions.

"Occupation: chemist."

Well, thought Petersen, a scientist. Maybe that was the explanation. Science makes a man old and keeps him young at the same time. But he was still bothered.

He stamped the passport and handed it back. "Thank you, Mr. Parker. I hope you enjoy your vacation in Denmark." And the moment he pronounced the name he knew that he had heard it before. Heard or seen it somewhere. Whitney C. Parker. But when and where he could not recall.

He was pretty sure that it had been mentioned in connection with an official matter; nevertheless he checked his papers and, of course, there was nothing that referred to it. How then did he know it? I'm getting old, thought Petersen. If a man can't remember correctly any longer . . . He shook his head to himself in disapproval, then, without quite knowing why, he made a little mark on the sheet onto which he had carried over Whitney Parker's data.

Whitney was still smiling as he left customs and walked down the narrow corridor toward the lobby. Momentarily he had forgotten the strenuous rush of the last days before he had been able to comply with Ørsted's appeal, the tiring flight from New York to Prestwick to Copenhagen. Nor did he think of the work ahead. All he felt was the happy anticipation of seeing Anders Ørsted within a minute or two.

When Anders had left America in 1950, both had thought that it would be only a little while until they would meet again. Instead, two and a half years had elapsed. "Science is like a prison," Anders had written once when Whitney had had to cancel a visit at the last moment. "And you're in for life. I know. Let's hope for another time." The time was now.

The lobby was crowded. Danish voices, high and shrill with excitement, mingled with English, French, German. Children yelled, a baby screamed, a piece of luggage dropped to the ground somewhere with a bang. Doors slammed, a telephone rang incessantly, and from outside came the tooting of buses. Whitney, only dimly aware of what was going on around him, was concentrating as hard as he could to catch, in the cacophony of noises, Anders' voice, to see the milling crowd fall back before the giant figure of his friend.

He waited in vain.

With a feeling of disappointment, Whitney watched the lobby empty. He sat down on one of the benches, searching his pockets for the lighter he always misplaced. It was a cheap little lighter and he had had it for many years, but then he liked things only after they had been in his possession for a long time and he was thoroughly used to them. Besides, Anders had given it to him in London, where they had first met during the war. Where was Anders? Always so incredibly punctual that, in the beginning of their friendship, Whitney's tendency often to be a bit late had been a source of irritation to Ørsted. Whitney smiled a little as he thought that now, for once, it was his turn to be annoyed. Then the smile died on his lips. That Anders should be late on an occasion like this seemed odd. You did not ask your friend, or anybody, to drop what he was doing at a moment's notice, go through the whole tedious business of obtaining a leave of absence, all sorts of permits and necessary papers, to let him hang around the airport of a strange country. Not Anders. Never Anders.

"In mutual interest come as soon as possible." They had used the phrase as a code for dangerous operations during the war. In his tired mind it began to repeat itself, like a tune you can't get rid of, until it sounded like a cry for help, and though Whitney knew that the only help that was wanted was his knowledge and experience in his special field of explosives, he grew unreasonably nervous. Nonsense, nonsense, he told himself. Probably Anders, absorbed in his work, had never planned to meet him but had assumed that Whitney would at once come out to the Holger Chemical Works.

The second this idea crossed his mind, it seemed beyond the realm of possibility that Anders, for sentimental reasons, should waste valuable time. Again Whitney recalled the text of the cable and the feeling of excitement that had rushed through him when he first read it. Something of great importance was happening somewhere in a quiet laboratory and he had been idiotic enough to . . .

There was a row of telephones attached to the wall without the privacy of a booth or any kind of partition. To his surprise Whitney heard himself ask for a connection with the Holger Works in Danish. He had picked up the language during the years he knew Anders and thought he had forgotten it long ago.

After a minute or so, the impersonal voice of a girl answered. "Good afternoon. Holger and Son, Chemical Works."

"Dr. Ørsted, please."

There was a click and a pause, then another voice, a soft, quiet voice which undoubtedly belonged to Ulla Rasmussen, Anders' elderly private secretary. He had met her in America that beautiful summer of '49. And with a flash, memory came back and in his mind's eye Whitney did not see her, but the long, handwritten letters Anders had received with unfailing regularity, intimate accounts about Anders' father who wouldn't let his son know how seriously ill he was. Whitney remembered the last one particularly. "You'd better come home," Ulla had written. "I don't want to sound too pessimistic but . . ." The week after that, Anders had left.

"Frøken Rasmussen," said Whitney, "this is Whit speaking, Whit Parker," and felt unreasonably relieved when he heard her warm acknowledging response. "I just got in. I'm calling from Kastrup. Yes. Can you put Anders on?"

"Anders? Isn't he with you?"

"No. That's why I'm calling. I thought he . . ."

"But I can't understand that," said the voice, and it sounded puzzled and a little upset. "He planned to meet you. Of course he did. He told me so yesterday when I called him on the farm. He's been working out there all week but he meant to drive in. Maybe something happened at the last moment to prevent it. There must be a message at the airport."

Of course there would be a message, and in the rush of three or more planes arriving, one after another, they had forgotten to page him. He had not thought of that.

"And if there isn't, what do you suggest I do? Come out to the Holger Works, call at Farimagsgade, or drive out to the country?"

"Oh no," came the answer. "Anders reserved a room for you at the Palace Hotel. I think you'd better go there and wait till you hear from me. I'll call the farm right away."

Whitney was immensely startled. He knew that Anders lived on the farm where he had been born, near Helsingør, about twenty-five miles north of Copenhagen, that he had a private laboratory out there in which he worked whenever his presence was not needed at the factory, and that he had a small bachelor apartment in Vestern Farimagsgade to make himself independent of commuting. It had never occurred to Whitney that he would not be a guest in one of Anders' homes, but he managed to push a sudden uneasiness out of his mind and ask the question he had wanted to ask from the beginning. "Is Helge around?"

Now the secretary laughed. "Yes," she said, "but don't call her. Don't spoil it. You're meant as a sort of surprise, Herre Parker."

That's why, thought Whitney. That's why Anders reserved a room for me at a hotel. Because of Helge.

All uneasiness left him. How thoughtful of Anders—Frøken Rasmussen, he corrected himself—to think that he might want a rest and to wash up before he was taken to the farm. Forgetting to inquire for a message, he strode out of the lobby and into the warm sunshine outside, smelling the wind from the stretch of blue sea to his left and the fragrance of flowering meadows all about him. The last bus for the city was leaving and he had to run for it. Helge, he thought. Helge.

As they drove through wide-open country toward Copenhagen, he looked neither to right nor left but back into the past. Four years ago he had met Helge, Anders' sister, who, with her father and Frøken Rasmussen, had come to visit her brother in America. And after a week-end spent at the Skytop in the Poconos, he had told Anders, "I think I'm going to marry her."

"God help her," Anders had answered. "Really, Whit, I mean it. Men like you and I are not cut out to make good husbands. Let her marry someone who's got time for a wife and a family, not such a lone wolf as you and I have to be." And then he had grown serious. "She's only a child, Whit. Just seventeen. Don't turn her head. She wouldn't know what she was doing if she said yes."

For a little while then their friendship had seemed less intimate. Whitney had not been sure whether Ørsted did not like him well enough to have him for a brother-in-law or whether he really believed that scientists were apt to make their wives unhappy. Then, watching Anders' devotion to his work and gradually getting so involved himself that every hour spent away from the lab seemed a waste of time, he came to realize how lonely and lost a woman might feel married to a man in love with science. Neither Anders nor he had married. Now Helge was a child no longer but twenty-one years old, and since she kept house for her brother, she should be well aware by now of what life with a man in their profession meant.

They were in the city now. Pink, thought Whitney. A pink city. For years he had tried to picture this old, old capital and somehow, knowing as much about it as he did, he had been convinced that he imagined it correctly. Yet it was one thing to have formed an image —to have heard or read that the Danes had started using brick as early as the twelfth century—but it was quite different actually to see the warm rose of buildings, like a special, soft illumination, light up the whole city. It also was quite different to see the green-blue copper of roofs on a colored photograph from seeing, in reality, what the material and its colors did to the sky. They separated and drew it close at the same time, becoming part of it like the green of an evening sky.

With the satisfaction of a child that has learned his lesson well, Whitney watched the gulls diving, the old-fashioned streetcars with their tiny white curtains blowing, the hundreds of people riding their bicycles with the graceful ease with which, in other countries, men and women balanced huge loads on their heads. But this is lovely, he thought, much lovelier than Anders or any book ever made it sound. And suddenly a hope, so alien that it surprised him, rose in him, the hope that he would have time before leaving to wander idly about this city, through all its sections and castles and parks and museums, really to get acquainted with Copenhagen and Denmark.

"*Raadhuspladsen,*" called the driver, who from time to time had pointed out a famous building or statue as though anything of sightseeing interest were his own specialty that he wanted to advertise. A moment later the bus stopped at the Palace Hotel on the Town Hall Square.

Somehow Whitney had traveled little—he didn't think of his two years in the air corps as travel—and rarely had he stayed at such an elegant hotel. While he showered and shaved, he enjoyed the luxury of the large old-fashioned room, then suddenly he was very tired and threw himself on the wide, comfortable bed. But the moment he stretched out, sleep eluded him. Everything combined to keep him awake. At any minute Anders might call for him. Whatever was of "mutual interest" would finally be explained. He would see Helge, be able to find out for himself if there were someone in her life or if she was still without any particular ties, and besides, beyond his open window, there was a strange city to be explored.

He dressed, went downstairs and discovered that a side-street café was part of the hotel. It seemed a good idea to sit out there, order a drink and watch the life on the square instead of wandering around, taking the chance that he might miss Anders. There was a newspaper stand in the entrance with the London *Times* and the Paris edition of the New York *Herald Tribune* prominently displayed. There were Swedish, French, Italian and German papers, and just as Whitney reached for a German magazine—he hadn't seen one for a long time—a man came in with a bundle of Danish papers, fresh from the press.

At first Whitney thought he'd make a mistake, that the face he saw in the left-hand corner, directly under the headline, was there only because he had been seeing it in his mind for hours; then he told himself that

15

there was no reason why Anders' photograph shouldn't be on the front page of a newspaper. After all, Anders Ørsted was known for his work far beyond the borders of his native country. Then Whitney's mouth went dry the way it always did in moments of shock or unbearable tension. His eyes refused to focus, his brain to work precisely. All knowledge of Danish left him. He could not make out the headline.

His voice sounded strangely angry when he turned to the girl behind the stand. "What does it say there?" he asked. "What does it say? For God's sake tell me what they say about him."

The girl looked at him, appalled, then at his shaking hand pointing to the picture. Her lips moved silently as she read to herself. "I hope he wasn't a friend of yours," she said finally in a shrill little voice, speaking English now as well as she could. "For he's dead. Drowned, it says. They found his boat with his clothes, drifting near the Swedish coast. But not his body. No sign of his body. It may take weeks or months till they find it. If ever. He used to bathe often from the boat, they write here. Perhaps a cramp. Perhaps the heart. Oh, how young he was. Only thirty-four. I'm sorry, sir."

She looked up but the foreigner had gone.

They are all alike, thought the girl angrily. They take it for granted that one speaks their language. They never trouble to learn the language of the countries they visit. But then, why should they? Half the world speaks English, only I wasn't born in that half and it took me a long time to learn it. The name of Anders Ørsted and his death meant nothing to her.

Not quite an hour later Whitney was driving along Route 3, going steadily north in the direction of Helsingør. His mind, numbed to the point where it resisted emotion, nevertheless demanded some physical activity. He simply had not been able to face the idea of sitting in the back seat of a taxi with nothing to do but wait for the driver to get him to Helge.

It had been no small feat to rent a self-driving car at an hour when places were closing, but this was what Whitney had achieved after his futile attempt to reach Ulla Rasmussen at the office, which no longer answered, and Helge Ørsted in the country, where the telephone had either been disconnected or was out of order. And when he had tried to ring Ulla Rasmussen's private number a repeated buzzing had told him she was not at home.

In Lingby he slowed down, for here, a mile or so from the road he was taking, lay the Holger Works. But what was the use of stopping there when he knew the factory was already closed for the night? He drove on, past Sorgenfri, the summer residence of the King, through Holte, surrounded by its beautiful forest, through Horsholm, where the wife of Christian VII had lived in scandalous love with Struensee, but the beauty of the countryside no longer meant anything to him and the little old towns failed to touch his sense of history.

Three days ago Anders had sent him the cable that had brought him here. It could only mean that Anders, in the course of some important work, had been stumped by something he had hoped Whitney could solve.

Speeding along the rather narrow highway, almost empty at this time of day, Whitney could feel the air getting fresher with a breeze from the sea, the sea which had taken Anders' life. Anders had been an exceptionally good swimmer. Perhaps a cramp, the paper had said. Cramp, thought Whitney. Other people drowned because of cramp. Why did it seem so odd? How do I know, Whitney asked himself, how tired he was, how many weeks, how many nights he may have worked without rest? It was a coincidence that Anders had drowned just on the day of his arrival.

There were coincidences. In Anders' own words, life was nothing but the coincidence of millions and millions of tiny facts. Then, still not permitting himself to think of his friend's death in personal terms, Whitney began to wonder what it was Anders could have hit upon and if he would be able to take over Anders' work.

He came to a crossing where he had to turn left to reach the Ørsted farm. It stood out in the flat open country like a primitive old fort. Four equally long and high wings with thatched roofs joined to form a perfect square. Dark heavy beams interrupted the whitewashed walls at regular intervals. But from where Whitney was approaching he could see no light. A car, though, stood in the drive, blocking the way, left there carelessly by somebody who had not bothered to park it properly.

Whitney crossed a stretch of lawn and as he came up to the house, shaded by enormous beeches, all his repressed feelings broke loose suddenly and unexpectedly, and he put his hand against the dark brown wood of the large gatelike entrance door to brace himself. How differently he had imagined it all.

There was a ship's bell over the door and after a while Whitney pulled its weathered cord and the bell rang out high and clear. And as he listened to its sound, he heard its echo answering from somewhere to the right, frail and forlorn. Then it was an echo no longer but a voice, Anders' voice. "Come as soon as possible . . . as possible . . . possible. . . ."

Whitney swung around as if, indeed, Anders had spoken to him, cried out in fear, a fear which the words of his cable had never transmitted. Had Anders been afraid for his life?

No, he thought. No. That's crazy. I've no reason to

assume . . . And then he knew that this thought had been at the back of his mind all along, remembered the rush of premonition when he had failed to find Anders waiting for him at the airport, the uneasiness which had assailed him when Ulla Rasmussen had prevented him from coming out to the Holger Works and sent him instead to the Palace Hotel. "In mutual interest." Whenever they had used the phrase during the war it had meant an operation that involved risk of life. Had Anders used it in that sense this time, too, not just as an indication that the United States might have a strong interest in his present work, as Whitney had surmised? Was Anders' death no accident?

His mind spinning, Whitney kept staring at the door, realizing only after a little while that it had remained closed. He rang again, rang without letting go of the cord so that the whole air was filled with the sound of the bell. Finally the door opened.

An old man, a green apron across his stomach, addressed him angrily. "Have you gone out of your mind, sir? That bell is rung only in case of fire. And we are not receiving strangers at this time of evening."

In the light flooding from the long narrow hall which had once been a stable, Whitney saw the doorbell he hadn't noticed before. He looked back at the man. It could only be Niels, the old servant. "I'm sorry," he said. "I'm Whitney Parker. Niels, will you tell Miss Helge that I'm here."

His name, he could see, meant nothing to Niels. Once more Whitney was sharply reminded how much, in his loneliness, he had adopted Anders Ørsted and his life as part of his own.

"Frøken Ørsted is not seeing anyone tonight."

"I know, I know," said Whitney and, realizing that Niels would not let him enter but would try to protect the privacy of his young mistress' grief, he stepped past him into the hall and through the door opposite the entrance into a flower-filled courtyard. "Helge," he cried. "Helge."

"I must ask you," said Niels's voice behind him, "to leave the house." But then another voice broke in. "It's all right, Niels."

Before Whitney stood Ulla Rasmussen, as plump, as gray-haired, as motherly as Whitney remembered her. "You've heard, of course," she said. "I tried to reach you but you had left the hotel. And I couldn't wait. My first duty was to Helge." Her voice wavered, grew steady again. "Come in here, please."

Whitney followed her into the living room. "How is she?"

"Helge? In a state of shock. She hasn't cried since she was told."

She sat down on a couch in front of an empty fireplace and buried her face in her hands and Whitney felt that this was the first time since the news had broken that Ulla Rasmussen was letting herself go. "She really raised us," Anders had told him. "Helge particularly. Our mother died a week after Helge's birth. I was just thirteen."

Whitney put his arm around the secretary's shoulder and after a little while she took her hands away from her face and pressed his hand. "I can't grasp it yet," she murmured. "It came too suddenly, too unexpectedly. I'm sorry, Mr. Parker. I know you must feel the same way. Anders used to say you were like brothers."

"When did you hear it?"

"The editor of the paper called me," she said. "He thought I knew. You see, they found the boat only around noon, near the Swedish coast. His clothes were in it and his wallet was in his jacket so they had no difficulty in identifying him. Besides, there was the number of his boat. They notified the Danish police and when the police checked . . ."

"But isn't it strange," he interrupted her, "that Anders should have thought of boating when . . . ?" He had meant to go on but suddenly it seemed impossible to add to her grief the horrid suspicion of murder.

"What do you mean, strange? Not at all. Anders often commuted by boat. This house is only three miles from the sea and during the summer months he frequently took the boat instead of the car or the train. And that's what he did today. We don't know exactly when he left but he always rose early."

"Why didn't the police phone his office? Notify you?"

"They phoned the house but Helge had gone to visit friends at Hornbaek, and Niels answered. And right after that the wire went dead. You see, we had a storm last night which lasted well into the early morning and they were repairing the lines around here."

"The telephone is still out of order."

She shook her head. "I had it disconnected. Too many calls were coming in." A sob escaped her. "The papers phoned a second after you'd hung up and then Niels's call came through and I told him not to say anything to Helge, I'd be out. I left immediately."

"Frøken Rasmussen," said Whitney, and now for the first time he sat down. He sat next to her, looking at her intently and seriously. "How much did Anders mention to you about his latest experiments in explosives?"

His tone of voice, his words, the concentration in his eyes, startled her. "I don't know what you mean," she said. "You know as well as I that when Anders had to take over his father's factory, he had to switch from his former field. Quite often, in the beginning at least, he used to say he regretted the fact that pharmaceutical chemistry took all his time."

"But he continued working with explosives out here. He must have."

"Not lately."

Whitney stared at her, completely at a loss. "But then why did he ask me to come?"

Ulla Rasmussen was equally astonished. "He asked you to come?"

"He cabled me," Whitney told her, "to come as soon as possible. That's why I'm here. Of course I thought it must have something to do with explosives."

"I don't understand it," she said. "I always thought I knew everything he did. I took care of all his private affairs, his mail. He must have sent the cable himself and forgotten to tell me about it. He never mentioned it. He only showed me your cable. 'Arriving Wednesday. Scandinavian Airlines.' Naturally I thought you had finally managed . . ."

Whitney's eyes narrowed abruptly. He had taken for granted that Ulla Rasmussen would at least know that Anders had summoned him. There must have been an important reason for Anders not to confide in this trusted old friend. Or had Anders, absorbed in his work, really merely forgotten to mention it as Ulla had suggested? Perhaps he was crazy to suspect foul play just because Anders had used a phrase that had once meant danger and had suffered a fatal accident on the day of his arrival.

"I guess he simply forgot."

Ulla Rasmussen shook her head. "No," she said. "No. He never forgot anything, not even unimportant details. He didn't want me to know. . . ."

Her voice trembled and Whitney realized that she was hurt. How like a woman, he thought, a mother who can't imagine that her children can keep secret from her any part of what they are doing or thinking. And how much like a woman in another respect—to be so offended that she does not even question the possible reasons behind Anders' secrecy. But, he told himself, if Anders had not wanted Ulla to know, had wanted her to believe that his friend was coming just for a vacation, there was no point in questioning her. She wouldn't know anything. And he didn't dare voice his suspicions before he had found something more substantial to justify them. Tomorrow there would be time to draw her out but tonight she was in no state to be of any use to him.

"Could I see Helge?" he asked.

She shrugged. "I told her you were here, hoping to get through to her, but she didn't react. She just said she didn't want to see anybody. Give her time. Wait till tomorrow, Herre Parker. I had Jytte get the guest room ready in case you want to stay with us. I wish you would."

They went out into the flower-filled little quadrangle

and into the right wing. Instead of following the style of most Danish houses in which the bedrooms were small, Anders had done a modern job when he turned the stables into living quarters. The room was wide and airy with French windows opening out onto the courtyard and two small windows overlooking the fields. There was a bowl of fruit on the table next to his bed. Ulla Rasmussen stopped short. "I never thought of offering you anything."

"Don't worry," Whitney said. "I'm not hungry."

"The kitchen is just across from your room," she said, "in case you change your mind. In the left wing. Anders said to get all sorts of things in because you liked to raid the icebox. Oh, Herre Parker . . ." And, the tears streaming down her face, she ran out of the room. Whitney heard her feet hurrying along the flagstone path and the sound of a door closing. He sat down on the bed, wondering if she would return or if this were her final good night.

He must have dozed off, for when he lifted his head the next time the house was deadly still and the lights which had shone out into the court before had been extinguished. He glanced at his watch. It was twenty minutes past midnight. He had left Copenhagen around six o'clock and, not knowing his way through the suburbs had needed an hour to get to the Ørsted farm. He had no recollection of how long exactly it had taken for

Niels to open the door. With the terrible suspicion rising in him, it had seemed as long as an eternity and as short as a second. But he could not have talked more than half an hour to Ulla Rasmussen. He must have slept about five hours. He didn't know why it was important to figure out all this but it was. For he could not help feeling that he had wasted a dreadful amount of time.

He took off his shoes and tiptoed through the court into the hall. The front door was locked. Two heavy iron bars, a yard apart, made it impossible to open it from the outside. Whitney didn't know that this door was hardly ever bolted and that only tonight Jytte, who believed in ghosts and devils, had sneaked out to bolt it when everybody was asleep. Whitney slid the bars carefully through their holders. Avoiding any noise, he put them down on the red-tiled floor of the hall and opened the door.

A quarter-moon swam in the sky, lending the night a strange, luminous quality, neither dusk nor twilight but a mixture of the two. "About one and a half miles down toward the sea," Anders had written, "I have converted an old barn into a lab." It was this lab toward which Whitney headed now.

He passed a cluster of small and big farm buildings until, on a lonely field, he could see the contours of the lab. He was prepared to smash a window to gain entry but to his surprise the door was not even locked. He switched on the light and found himself in his accustomed surroundings. There were all the beakers, flasks, tubes, funnels, graduates, burettes, crucibles, retorts, microscopes, all the equipment he had known since he had first decided to study chemistry. And there was drop test equipment. Anders must have gone on working in his former field, regardless of what Ulla Rasmussen said, for this apparatus was used to determine the sensitivity of explosives.

He glanced across the rows upon rows of dusty glass containers on shelves. As he stopped to read some of the labels he frowned with annoyance over Anders' habit of putting numbers instead of names on them. This made it impossible to determine the contents without a chart. As he walked around the room, his hands felt the empty spaces of the walls. Maybe there was a safe. But he could find none. He sat down at the work table which was incredibly tidy except for a coffee machine. That he was used to also. None of the drawers were locked but there were no samples, no notes, no charts, nothing that gave Whitney the slightest clue as to what Anders had been working on. Either Anders had locked all data of his work in a different place or somebody had thoroughly cleaned out whatever he had kept here.

Not knowing what to think or do in his disappointment, Whitney left the lab, and as he walked through the night he thought he heard, amid the chirp of crickets, another sound. Soft steps, as though somebody were walking behind him. He turned abruptly. The outline of a group of trees, the prone body of a cow— that was all. He walked on, listening. Now he could hear nothing. Perhaps he had imagined it or mistaken a hunting dog's soft paws for the sound of feet following him. As he rebolted the door of the house, he took off his shoes again and, shoes in hand, went into the living room, through the small library and crossed the dining room into the kitchen. It was tiled all the way around and the tiles, as the moonlight hit them, glittered softly like blue and purple ice. He went into the anteroom and hesitated for a second. Then, breathing deeply, he entered Anders' bedroom.

It was a large, almost bare room, its main piece of furniture a huge desk. There was one hard, one comfortable deep chair. A shelf of books on explosives over the head of the narrow bed. Beside it hung a map of Denmark.

Whitney stepped closer. In what a perilous geographical position these little Northern countries were. If Russia should ever decide to go to war, she would have to overrun this part of Europe as one of the key positions she needed to block any enemy fleet from sailing up the Baltic.

Whitney's attention was disrupted by a slight sound outside the room. It might have been anything. Nevertheless he went over to the windows and drew the curtains. Then he sat down at Anders' writing desk. He turned on the desk lamp, a student lamp they had bought together once in Pennsylvania. For a second he sat staring at it and memories filled him, choking him.

He had grown up an orphan on a lonely farm in New Jersey where distances had made it impossible for him to play with children except during recesses in the school that was fourteen miles from his house. Besides, he had been needed for work on the place and not until his uncle, a quiet silent man, died and to his surprise left all he had to him, did Whitney have a chance to mix with people. But by then he had formed a habit of being by himself. Discovering how much schooling he had missed, he had devoted himself to his studies. It had taken Anders and the war to break through his reserve.

Whitney did not feel indiscreet as he started to pull open the top drawer. This, he was sure, Anders would have wanted him to do, yet it was a strange feeling to see and touch what another man had entrusted to the privacy of his desk. Bundles of letters held together with a rubber band, photographs, bills, a diary. Whitney was opening the diary when a voice behind him said, "Don't move or I'll shoot."

He spun around. On the threshold stood a small figure dressed in a white bathrobe. Helge.

"Helge," he said, "Helge darling, it's only me."

The gun dropped to the floor. "Whitney," she cried, as if she could not trust her eyes. "Whit. And I thought I heard a burglar."

For a second her eyes lighted up, her mouth curved in an unconscious smile, and Whitney rose, forgetting for a moment the dreadful circumstances of this meeting, filled with a joy he had not thought possible. She hadn't changed, not a bit. She was exactly as he remembered her. Suddenly he could not understand how he could have let four years pass, how he could have been content to wait for what the future might bring instead of rushing to Europe to tell her. . . . He held out his arms and Helge made a step forward, as shy suddenly as he; then her eyes fell on the open desk and she drew back abruptly.

"What are you doing here? How dare you touch his things? Get out of his room. Immediately."

He longed to take her in his arms, to hold her close, but knew that he must not touch her now. He remained seated, wondering desperately how he could explain why he wasn't in his room but, in the dead of night, going through Anders' private things.

"I guess," he said, as though she had not ordered him angrily out of the room, "you would have shot if you had not recognized me in time. You gave me quite a start. Since when do you carry a gun?"

Like a distracted child, she bent and picked up the revolver. "Anders gave it to me," she said, " 'Just in case,' he said. It's his old revolver, the one he used in the war."

Whitney did not stir. "When did he give it to you?"

For a moment it seemed hard for her to remember. "Yesterday," she said. "I think it was yesterday. Or the day before. He was opening his safe when I came in and he took it out and said, 'You might as well have it. Just in case.' "

Whitney sat very still. Yesterday, or the day before yesterday. Why should Anders have handed his sister a gun if he did not believe she might have to use it? He watched Helge cross the room toward him. She still moved with the quiet grace he remembered. Her hair, the color of polished brass, was still as long as it had been when she wore it in two heavy braids around her head. Now it was hanging open over her robe. He wanted to stretch out his hand and feel it but he saw her eyes—golden brown eyes such as Botticelli had painted. The anger with which she had spoken to him before showed in their glance again.

"You may have been his best friend," she said, "but I

find it disgusting to see you looking through his desk. You have no right to steal his notes. They're all that's left of him now. And I'm going to see to it that they're published under his name."

He looked at her in surprise. "What are you talking about? What in the world's got into you? You can't seriously . . ." He stopped and said very softly, "Who's been trying to steal Anders' notes?"

Helge sat down in the chair between desk and bed. "I don't know," she said. "I don't know. Forgive me. I guess Severin upset me. I had only just been told of Anders' death when he called, hardly bothering to be polite, and said he wanted Anders' notes on Project 11. He's always been jealous of Anders."

Severin. Severin. The name meant nothing to him. "Who is Severin?"

"But Anders must have told you about him, the brilliant young German he engaged last year?"

Then it came back to Whitney, the name and description Anders had given of Severin in one of his letters: "He's incredibly ambitious, but then ambition often lies at the root of great discoveries."

"What was Project 11?"

"You too," she said. "Well, I don't know. Ask Severin. Ask Ulla. Ah, this is cruel of you."

She rose and with one wide furious gesture swept the papers he had taken out back into the still open top drawer. But some of them fell to the floor. Severin, he thought. Perhaps Anders had trusted him. . . . There is a safe in this room. Helge mentioned it. Maybe she knows the combination.

Now, to gain time, he knelt on the floor and gathered up the papers that had fallen. And as he carefully picked them up, looking at each item quickly before he put it back on the desk, he could feel her watching him.

"I thought you loved him," she said, "almost as much as I did. But all you care about are his latest findings. Wasn't Anders on the trace of something even better than tuberculine? Wasn't Anders working on a new drug against leukemia? Just like everybody else, interested only in some sensational news about his work. But what about him, as a person, as a man?"

"Helge," he said, "would you open his safe for me? You know the combination, don't you?"

His question shocked her as he had intended it should, as he could not help shocking her. Her face went white and her voice was barely audible when she answered. "After all I've just told you, after I have just said how it hurts me that nobody seems to care about his death, only about what is left behind of his work, you of all people dare . . ."

Whitney got up and stood in front of her, barring her way. "Listen to me," he said. "Helge, listen. Anders

may have left something of great importance. And because I believe this so strongly, I cannot show you the
consideration I would like to. I need your help. Without your help I may never find out what it is. You see,
Helge," and now he spoke very slowly, very clearly, "I
am afraid that Anders was murdered."

It was a dreadful thing to say, a dangerous and
dreadful thing. Whitney realized it to its full extent
only when he voiced his suspicion. For a moment a
deep silence filled the room, a silence he did not dare
break; then Helge laughed, the odd little laughter of
beginning hysteria.

"Who should have murdered him?"

"Somebody who knew he had discovered something
important and wanted it."

"Who?" she asked again.

Yes, who? he thought. Staring past her at the wall
he again saw the map. He caught his breath. He had
not realized when he looked at it before how close the
Russians were to the Danish shore. Since Germany had
been divided, there were only a few miles between
Denmark and the Russian controlled German coastline.

"I don't know," he said. "Perhaps somebody in the
pay of Russian agents."

"You Americans!" she said. "You can't accept facts
for facts. You're the most scared people I've ever met.
You see ghosts around the corner, spies, communists.

Anders drowned. He swam from the boat and drowned. You don't know the current in The Sound. I do. It's terribly dangerous."

"He swam in The Sound all his life," said Whitney. "He knew it like his own pocket."

Helge stared at him. Now she was not laughing, not talking wildly. "Like his own pocket," she repeated. "But the police are satisfied."

"This afternoon, when I looked up the roads to take out here," said Whitney, "I looked at the waterways, too. If Anders went to Copenhagen as usual, why was his boat found on the Swedish coast? Does a boat drift across three miles that quickly? Wouldn't you say he went in the wrong direction?"

"Not if he went to Sweden," she said, frowning sharply. Then her lips began to tremble. "But he planned to be in Copenhagen early this morning."

Whitney sat down on the arm of the chair as though his physical presence might ease her terror. "Unfortunately," he said, "things like this have happened throughout the past years, justifying my fears. You are wrong if you think Anders did not share this constant awareness of danger. Every scientist does. He must. He has to imagine the future. And Anders did. He gave you his gun. Why do you think he wanted you to have a gun?"

36

"I thought it was a joke," she whispered, "or a token of affection."

"Maybe he wanted you to think that so you wouldn't be frightened."

She shivered, shaking her head to herself in silent struggle with the horrifying possibility. "There was a burglary two nights ago. Oh, nothing much. In his lab. Only his typewriter was taken. But burglaries are so rare here, he was quite upset. Maybe that's why . . ."

Only his typewriter, thought Whitney, or was that only what Anders had told her? Again he thought of the empty drawers, of the sound of steps. Perhaps he hadn't imagined them after all. And then he heard Helge crying, not wildly, not loudly, but softly. The first tears she had been able to shed since she heard of her brother's death.

For a while he said nothing, just let her cry; then, very quietly, he began to tell her about the cable and that Anders, knowing how difficult it would be for him to make this trip, would never have asked him unless his coming was absolutely necessary.

Helge stopped crying. "I know, Whit. I know. You're right. He would never have asked you otherwise, but oh . . . I don't want to believe it."

She threw her arms around him, pressing her face against his chest as though by turning her back on life

37

she could escape the horrors of their century. She felt warm and soft against him and Whitney put his hand on her hair, felt its silkiness and withdrew it abruptly.

How differently he had imagined their first embrace. Instead of happiness there were the tears of tragedy, the sister taking him as a substitute for the brother she had lost and he had to behave as brother and friend and forget the hours he had longed for her. This was not the time to tell her about his love.

"Let's see if we can find anything in the safe."

Helge straightened up. Her eyes were enormous. Without a further word of opposition she went to where the shelf hung over the bed. She pressed against some hidden mechanism behind the books and the shelf moved to reveal a steel box. A minute later she had emptied the safe and put its contents on the bed.

"That's all there is," she said. "It doesn't look like much."

Indeed it didn't. Strangely enough, except for the keys to a Copenhagen bank safe, there were mostly things one usually did not put in a safe. Photographs, for instance. Whitney remarked on it.

"He was always afraid of fire," said Helge.

She sat at the foot of the bed, her shoulders hunched, still trembling. Now she picked up some of the yellowing daguerreotypes. "My grandmother. My great-grandmother. My great-great-grandfather. Anders was the last of our name and so conscious of family history. He should have married, but he always claimed that it took a special girl to make a scientist's wife."

"He may still. . . ." Whitney bit his lip. He had spoken as though Anders were still alive, still able to find a companion.

But Helge had noticed it. "I can't grasp it either," she said. "Oh Whit, he meant everything to me."

Whitney stared down at the photo he was holding in his hand. His friendship with Anders had changed his whole life, more than that, his attitude toward life, his whole conception. Anders' courage had impressed him, his knowledge had made him want to reach the same level as Ørsted, his objectivity had helped Whitney to form his judgment. "This is what he looked like when I met him first," he said, "over ten years ago. You were a little girl then but at his quarters in London your picture was the only one. He used to worry that something might happen to you during his absence while we were worried stiff that he might get caught as a spy every time we dropped him back into Denmark."

Helge's hands trembled as she took the photo from him but somehow his mention of her brother's courage during the Occupation had given her strength. She was able to look at the picture without bursting into tears.

"There they are," she said, "all of them," and pointed to the pencil marks around some of the faces in a group picture. "I wasn't supposed to know what they were doing but of course I did, because I had known them all my life and I could tell by the way they behaved if anything was up or not. Iver and Eric and Frederick and little Ove. Mogens and Kai."

Whitney bent closer. Only one face besides Anders' seemed familiar. He had seen it somewhere but could not recall where. "Who's that?" he asked.

"Petersen. Ove Petersen," she said. "He used to be a passport control officer on a boat between Gedser and Germany. I wonder what happened to him."

Then suddenly Whitney knew where he had seen Petersen's face—at the Kastrup airport. But he did not want to interrupt her now when she was speaking freely for the first time. "Kai was shot," she said. "He was caught trying to derail a train. And Eric died smuggling some people to Sweden. And this is Mogens, who knows all the waters as well as his own back yard, the Baltic and the Skagerrak and the North Sea up to the Arctic. He never seemed to be in one place but in ten at the same time, drinking and gambling, a daredevil if ever there was one. And now he's bored with the peace."

Mogens' name rang familiar. Whitney searched his mind. Years dropped away and he was back in London.

Not everybody had trusted Mogens. Rumors had said that he was playing both sides to his own advantage, but Anders had always stood up for him, laughed at all warnings and relied on Mogens.

Helge was pointing to two men standing with their arms linked. "Of Iver and Frederick you must have heard Anders speak often."

"Iver Larsen, the lawyer?"

Helge nodded. There was the shadow of a smile in her eyes. Whitney noticed it with a quick feeling of jealousy. Perhaps it had been a mistake to let the years pass without telling her that he loved her.

"A pretty nice fellow," she said, "as far as lawyers go. Anders thought a lot of him." The smile vanished from her face and she sighed. "He will grieve as we do. It will come as a terrible shock to him."

Whitney thought of the moment when he had first spotted Anders' picture on the front page, how the foreign language he knew quite well had suddenly become indecipherable as in a nightmare. But the nightmare had become fact, a fact which, if his suspicions proved correct, involved not only the death of a friend but might carry far-reaching consequences for people who had never even known of Anders Ørsted's existence.

"He won't be back until tomorrow," said Helge. "He's in Paris right now."

Whitney took another look at the narrow handsome face. Again he asked himself if he meant more to Helge than just someone she had known for years. Then, as her finger pointed to Frederick Gabel, he remembered that this was not only a friend of the Ørsteds but also their doctor. Gabel might be able to tell him if Anders had been subject to cramps lately and Iver, as the Ørsteds' lawyer, might have been entrusted with matters Anders had not dared confide to Helge or Ulla Rasmussen. He would have to see all of them, these men who had been boys with Anders and become his closest friends after the war.

Photos, letters, a few cases of jewelry. An envelope with a small sum of money in cash. And nothing else. Whitney was putting it all back when he saw it, a piece of paper flattened against the side of the lining which Helge must have overlooked.

In Anders' writing, clear and even as a monk's, it said, "July 18, 1953. I herewith acknowledge payment of ten thousand kroner," and signed with blunt strokes was a name: "J. Mogens. Fisherman. Hornbaek."

Payment, thought Whitney. Payment, not a loan. Payment for something that wasn't mentioned. July 18th. It was the 23rd of July today. Anders' cable had been dated July 19th.

"What is Mogens doing now?" he asked.

"Mogens? What he is always doing. Fishing. Why?"

She caught some of Whitney's excitement and her hands flew to her heart. "What has he got to do with it? Whit, you're not suspecting him, are you? He'd never harm Anders."

"I didn't say that. Just tell me, were they still seeing each other?"

"But of course. Anders would always let Mogens take him out for tunny or to Jutland for the salmon fishing and sometimes he'd just go along for fun."

"Have you any idea for what Anders could have paid such a sum of money?"

"What sum?" She came over and took the slip of paper from Whitney and shook her head. "I can't imagine what this means. He never wanted to charge Anders even for the use of the boat."

"Do you think he might have needed money?"

"Oh, he always needed money. He bought a new boat this spring. Maybe Anders loaned him . . ." She interrupted herself, "But here it says payment. Payment for what? It doesn't make sense. There's nothing Mogens could have to sell at such a price."

Whitney's mind spun. Fifteen hundred dollars was a small fortune in this country. A new boat, he thought. But then Anders would have put it down, would have written loan instead of payment. There was something strange in the fact that Anders, so exact in all his affairs, should have omitted for what he had paid such a large sum. It had been left out purposely. But what could Mogens have to sell? What knowledge could a simple fisherman have gained that was worth ten thousand kroner, and why should he have turned to Anders unless this knowledge was of some special interest to a scientist? It seemed improbable though that a man with no scientific education should know something that could be of sufficient importance for Anders to buy. It was more logical to assume that he had been ordered to find out what Ørsted was working on, break into his lab and steal. . . .

Whitney closed his eyes. Ordered by whom? he thought. Who could possibly order Mogens to steal scientific data?

A daredevil, Helge had said, who knew the sea and its currents like his own back yard, bored with peace after having tasted the adventure of war. Had Mogens, to make life exciting once more, sailed his boat a little too far out of home waters and met up with the Russians?

There had been a burglary two nights ago. Nothing had been taken, Helge had said, except a typewriter, but Anders had been upset. What if Anders had caught Mogens in the act of robbing his desk and had paid him the sum of ten thousand kroner to find out who had ordered the fisherman to break into his laboratory? And had Mogens, perhaps, a day or two later, grown afraid of having betrayed his instigator and decided that Anders constituted a danger to him?

Helge was speaking again. "He killed fourteen Germans," she said, "single-handed. You see, Whit, you could not take prisoners. You either evaded the Germans or you had to kill them. Mogens always managed situations in which he had to kill even when it was unwise and would bring only retaliation on their part. But he hated the Germans, and he's got a dreadful temper when he's roused. He used to take their bodies out to sea and drown them so that they wouldn't be found and nobody would ever know. . . ." She broke off abruptly, trembling all over, her face white, her eyes dark with terror. "But why should he kill Anders? Why should Mogens kill Anders?"

CHAPTER TWO

There was the harbor.

Whitney stopped the car but remained seated behind the wheel and looked around. It was a small harbor; only about thirty boats lay at anchor. "He may stay out most of the night, he may leave before dawn and he may not have gone out at all," Helge had said, and added something about calling in the police. Whitney had gradually convinced her that it was too early and possibly inopportune to notify the authorities and then promised not to go without her to see Mogens. He had just broken this promise. Helge was finally asleep in her room and on the hall table he had left a letter of instructions for her in case he should not return.

Dawn was breaking fast and across The Sound the Swedish coast lost its dim outlines, became distinct, and Whitney could see the green of trees and white houses taking shape while directly in front of him the rising sun illuminated the names of the boats in the shelter of two long moles built of huge boulders.

He left his car and walked past the one-story building of a small fish market until he came to the spot where Elephant III had made fast. He did not know that the elephant was Denmark's national symbol and for a second he wondered why Mogens should have given this name to his cutter. But even as he wondered, he knew that he was paying attention to unimportant matters only to counteract his mounting tension.

A woman in heavy pants and a turtleneck sweater was throwing some garbage into the water which was greasy and dirty with orange peel and empty ice-cream cones and tins swimming around. The tide was not yet in. He asked her if Mogens was on his boat and she shrugged, but when he inquired where Mogens lived— he had not dared question Helge, afraid of betraying his intention to see the fisherman alone—the woman slowly and haughtily turned her back on him.

Whitney, after a moment's hesitation, jumped into a rowboat close to the quai and from there climbed over an American Chris-Craft, a small sailing boat and a trawler until he was able to swing himself onto the Elephant. There was only the faint odor of fish, otherwise everything was scrubbed spotlessly clean and it was obvious that Mogens had not been out this night. The door to the tiny wheelhouse was locked, no fishing tackle lay around and Whitney began to wonder where he might find the man he suspected of murder when, through the cabin door, he heard heavy snoring.

He had to knock several times before, with a curse, the door was opened. In front of him stood the figure of a huge man, naked but for a pair of faded denims. His blond hair was tousled and his very light and small eyes, heavy with sleep, showed no sign of curiosity for the stranger who had awakened him so abruptly. "I'm not going fishing today," he said, "I'm not taking anybody out," and he slammed the door.

Perhaps it was only in this instant that Whitney grew fully aware of the part he had assigned himself. Until he found Mogens he had acted like a man in his sleep, automatically driven to action by his suspicions. Now it occurred to him that he had never tried before to break down a man and that he might not be able to do it. A sudden fear assailed him that the only thing he might accomplish would be to put this man on his guard and, instead of solving anything, give him the chance to wipe out all possible traces. This was a job for a man experienced in matters like this, not for a scientist. Besides, all disadvantages were on his side. He was a stranger in this country.

He opened the door.

"Get out," Mogens shouted before Whitney had even put his foot into the cabin. "Get out. I told you I'm not going fishing today. Now git."

With the stubbornness which was a part of his

48

nature, blind once more to the possible danger that Mogens might attack him, Whitney entered. "Helge Ørsted asked me to see you."

Mogens was lying on his bunk. He did not stir. "Didn't want to see me last night," he said. "I went to the house the moment I heard it over the air. Wouldn't see me," he said again, shaking his head to himself and with something like anger in his eyes.

"She wouldn't see anybody," Whitney told him, holding out a pack of cigarettes to the man.

Mogens chose to overlook them. "She saw you."

"I happened to be there," Whitney lied. "I had just arrived from the States and gotten to the farm when the news came through."

He didn't know why he said it, why he revealed more than he had planned, but his instinct told him that he would never find out for what and how Mogens had received ten thousand kroner unless he could establish a basis for conversation.

To his surprise it worked. Mogens lifted his head and looked him over and Whitney could not remember ever having been scrutinized so sharply before. "You the guy he expected?"

Somehow it seemed incongruous that the fisherman should know about his coming. Whitney nodded. "Yes. I'm Whitney Parker."

"That's the name," said Mogens. "Easy to remember.

I always did because of the Parker pen. Learned that in the war, to associate names with things and numbers with colors. Well, sit down. I'm glad she sent you."

Whitney looked startled. How good an actor was this man that he could sound so convincing? He sat down on the bunk opposite Mogens and watched Mogens busy himself in the small galley at the far end of the cabin. "Couldn't eat last night," he said. "Guess you couldn't, either. But a man has to go on living and in order to live he's got to eat. Felt the same way when my wife died a couple of years ago, so I know you can't bring back the dead by starving."

He took a couple of plates and cups from a rack and a moment later brought a battered blue-enamel pot and a pan with fried eggs to the table that was nailed to the floor between the four bunks. *"Velbekome,"* he said, and began to eat ravenously. And while he ate, his eyes intent on the food before him, he did not speak.

There was something sly about those light blue eyes which seemed as faded as his denims by the sun and salt air. *"Velbekome,"* he said again when they had finished and Whitney found that, in spite of his tension, he had eaten everything he was offered. And then Mogens leaned back, his head level with the porthole so that the light made his hair seem like that of an old man, silver white, pulled out his tobacco pouch and

50

lighted his pipe. And while he did so, his eyes, small and cunning, were on Whitney's face.

Whitney remained silent. Let him speak, he thought. There is no greater temptation for a man whose conscience is burdened than to break an ominous silence. He was right. He hadn't smoked half his cigarette when Mogens asked, "Why did Frøken Helge send you?"

"Just to give you the message that she wanted to see you."

"What for?"

"I don't know, but I guess she wanted to find out when you last saw her brother."

"Hm," said Mogens, noncommittally. But after a moment's pause he bent forward and put his strong muscular arms on the table between the dirty dishes. "Tell you what," he said. "Tell you what, Herre Parker. I don't believe it was an accident."

Whitney drew back as though he had suddenly stepped on a poisonous snake. What had made this man decide to be the first to attack? But then, wasn't sudden attack supposed to be one of the most stupefying weapons? Was this simple fisherman clever enough to cast the suspicions he might feel threatening him onto somebody else?

"What in the world makes you say that?"

"It came to me," said Mogens, speaking very slowly,

as though he wanted Whitney to understand every word, "when I was bicycling along, came to me when she didn't want to see me, on my way home. Mogens, I said to myself, that Anders could swim like a trout. He wouldn't drown like a sack of flour. If he felt a cramp coming on he'd just lie low, motionless, like a fish."

"I understand Dr. Gabel warned Anders to take it easy."

It was fantastic that their parts should be reversed, that he should be trying to convince this man that Anders' death was accidental when he had just spent hours convincing himself it was murder.

"Gabel can't swim," said Mogens, shrugging away any medical opinion.

"The police seem to be satisfied."

"Sure," said Mogens. "Any man who makes extra work for himself is a fool."

"They even think it's possible that his boat should have drifted to the Swedish coast."

"It didn't drift."

"How do you know?"

"Because I know," said Mogens. "I know that boat and I know the currents."

"Then what's your explanation?"

"He came from Sweden," answered Mogens, and

now for the first time Whitney saw him smile, an odd little smile he couldn't figure out.

"You sound damn sure."

"I'm not," said Mogens. "I just think it's the only explanation. He came from Sweden."

"Why should he have come from Sweden?"

"Because he often went there, to Helsingborg."

"What did he do there?"

Mogens put an enormous hand on Whitney's. "Look, Herre Parker, he didn't tell me all he did. Maybe there was a girl. All I'm trying to tell you is that I don't believe it was an accident."

"Have you talked to anybody about your suspicions?"

Mogens took his hand away and shook his head. "I wanted to," he said. "I went to Gabel's house but he was out on a call and his wife didn't know when he would be back. Then I tried Larsen. He was away, in France, they told me."

Whitney straightened, getting himself into a position where a sudden blow would not find him unprepared. "Then I think we should call in the police."

"No," said Mogens, a little too quickly, his eyes mere slits in his brown, brutal face. "You leave the police out of this."

"I'm afraid I can't. Don't you see . . . ?"

Mogens' move found Whitney ill-prepared after all.

53

Before he could get up, Mogens was standing over him, pinning him down. "Sorry," he said, "but you Americans are always so impatient. Just forget about the police, Herre Parker, and listen to me. And don't think you can fool around with the police, because I won't let you." He loosened his grip and with one step crossed over to the door, blocking it with his huge body.

Whitney felt for the gun Anders had given to Helge, which he had taken along. "They broke into Ørsted's lab two days ago," he said. "What do you know about that, Mogens? How do you explain the ten thousand kroner you were paid by Ørsted?"

The muscles around Mogens' chin tightened and Whitney pulled out the gun. "I think you'd better come along."

To his surprise, Mogens began to laugh, full loud laughter. Throwing back his head, he seemed unable to stop laughing and Whitney asked himself if this was a new trick or the hysteria of a criminal who knew he was trapped. After a while Mogens' laughter ebbed away and when he spoke there was no trace of amusement in his voice.

"So you suspected foul play all along," he said. "And you figured when you heard about the money that I had something to do with it. Well, I didn't want that money to begin with. Anders forced it on me. He even made me sign a paper. That's Anders for you. He wouldn't think of it as a present."

"Think of what as a present?"

Mogens gave him a long look. "Don't know if I should tell you," he said, "when you're stupid enough to think I killed him." He moved his head slowly from side to side as if the sound of the word "kill" were one he could not grasp. "1941, it was," he said, "when three men volunteered to have themselves dropped from British planes into Denmark. The first man was captured and shot on the spot, Anders and I got through. Nobody was expecting us and nothing was organized but we two . . ." He interrupted himself, closing his eyes. When he looked up again his glance fastened on Whitney with queer intensity.

"Maybe you aren't such a blockhead after all," he said, "only Anders wanted it kept a dead secret and if I ever find you talking . . ." and to his complete bewilderment, Whitney saw two big tears running slowly down the tanned, unshaven cheeks. "I've got something to do with it," said Mogens, letting the tears fall unashamed. "At least, I think I do. That's why I almost feel like a murderer. You see, I found something. I went out fishing as usual last Sunday and when I brought in my net, the sun hit something that didn't look like a fish. It looked like a tin. Only it was heavy.

And stamped into the steel cap was a number, U-247. Now you know, perhaps, that some of the Nazis tried to get away in submarines. . . ."

At once odds and ends came to Whitney's mind, things he had heard and read, about German subs trying to escape to the Argentine. Quite recently there had been an article about two which had exploded in Danish waters years ago. They were supposed to be the ones that had carried with them the latest German invention of a new explosive but they ran into a depth charge and all evidence was assumed to have been destroyed.

A different kind of tension from that which he had felt on his way to Mogens rose in Whitney. He tried to light a cigarette, then, as though he couldn't be bothered, just let it hang between his lips.

"Things came up from time to time," said Mogens, "parts of a tower, pieces of a bridge, steel splinters, bodies no longer identifiable, tarnished medals, all sorts of things, and now there was this tin. I opened it, which wasn't easy, and what was in it was a powder, white like sugar. There was a piece of paper in the cap which said, 'Sample.' And that was all. I took it to Anders."

Whitney's mouth went dry and his voice was harsh. "Go on. Did Anders say anything?"

"Yep. He said how lucky for us that it hadn't been found in Russian waters. And suddenly he made me swear not to breathe a word of this to anybody. And then he insisted on paying me. I wouldn't hear of it but he said it was worth a small fortune to him."

Whitney sat motionless. There was a strange satisfaction in having been right about the reasons for Anders' cable. But Ulla Rasmussen's information had been correct, too. Anders had not worked on explosives lately, but had cabled Whitney because, by pure chance, he had come across the container. A fortune. Worth a fortune to Anders, to the United States, to the Russians. Whitney looked at Mogens and suddenly all his suspicions of the man dropped away. There was no proof, yet he was sure that Mogens was speaking the truth. He felt intensely embarrassed.

"I didn't speak to anybody," Mogens said, "but there were the hands, Bertel and Kristen. They knew, of course, that we'd fished something out of the sea that had belonged to a former Nazi sub. You don't think right away of being careful or that it might be something important. And I didn't want to tell the boys to keep their mouths shut. They might have wondered why such a fuss was being made about a little steel container." He smiled at Whitney. "You still believe, Herre Parker, that I broke into Anders' place, stole the container and sold it to the Russians, don't you? Well, if you do, there's nothing I can do about it. It's up to you to recognize a man for what he is or isn't."

Whitney shook his head. "I made a mistake," he said. "I'm sorry." He held out his hand and Mogens clasped it.

All his assumptions concerning this man, he thought, had proved wrong, yet his suspicions about the money paid to Mogens had led him to the heart of the matter. He looked at Mogens. "But why," he asked, "why do you speak as if the Russians knew about it?"

"Not the Russians themselves," said Mogens, "but their agents. We've got quite a few communists here. We worked hand in hand with them during the Occupation. Some are openly members of the Party, some secretly, however the tide runs. But I know that last year a very important formula was stolen from the Holger Works and that Anders was worried that something might happen to him."

Vestern Farimagsgade.

It was not a quiet street but then, it was close to the center of Copenhagen. A tram ran through it, bicycle bells rang shrilly and horns tooted. Whitney looked up at the red-brick building and then back at his map. From here it was only a few blocks to the railroad station, equally close to the Tivoli and in convenient walking distance to the Raadhuspladsen. Anders had always liked contrast and found stimulation in the dif-

58

ferences of things. The serenity of the country versus
the hubbub of a city, the undisturbed concentration of
the mind against the concentration on physical move-
ment. This modern apartment house was just another
proof that Anders had not changed.

Whitney went up two flights of stairs and past several doors until he came to the one marked "24." Helge
had given him the key and as he inserted it he wondered if here, perhaps, he would find the container or
some clue as to where it might be hidden, or some notes
Anders might have made. Unable to curb his impatience, he had told Helge about his visit to Mogens as
soon as he had returned to the farm and had begged
Helge to come with him to Copenhagen. Only she had
the authority to demand the bank keys and open the
safe. Now he wished he hadn't insisted.

It had upset her terribly. For more than an hour they
had gone carefully through all the papers and discovered nothing, not a note, not a chart referring to the
explosive. But there, in a big manila envelope, they had
found his will. And, "I can't stand it," Helge had said.
"I know this is important, Whit, but I can't take it. I
can't take it that life is going on as if nothing had
happened, that trams run and guards clink their keys
and people eat and drink and go about their business.
. . . I'm sorry, Whit, but you'll have to go to his apart-

59

ment by yourself. I don't want to hear anything or do anything. I want to be left alone. I'm going back to the farm."

And he had let her go without seeing her home. He couldn't sit with her and talk to her and soothe her. There was no time for that. Iver Larsen, he thought, just home from Paris, might take his place, might at this very moment be driving up to the house, and he envied the lawyer the intimacy of shared grief.

A small hall, not bigger than a closet, a living room, a dining room, one opening into the other and with all the doors standing ajar, allowing him to see into the bedroom.

He felt the presence of the man before he actually saw him. Like Whitney the night before, he was hastily searching Anders' desk in the small bedroom. For just a moment Whitney stood frozen to the floor, then he rushed forward.

The man was so intent on what he was doing, he didn't hear Whitney until he felt hands closing around his throat. Then, struggling to move his head, he tried to speak. "Let go," he said. "At once, you fool."

This was not the reaction Whitney had expected. He loosened his grip, and the man spun around and faced him. "Who the hell are you?" he said. "And what are you doing here?"

Whitney, keeping the man pinned back in the chair,

60

saw a dark, intelligent face, deep brown eyes with a burning intensity in their glance, a thin-lipped mouth with teeth so stained and crooked they betrayed insufficient nourishment and endless smoking. "That's what I was going to ask you."

"I'm Otto Severin," the man said, and it sounded bored. "I thought you were the caretaker, come to see if everything was all right in here or on some kind of errand. Now take your hands off me."

Otto Severin, thought Whitney. Anders' import from Germany.

He stepped back and Severin leaned forward in his chair across a pile of papers which had fallen back onto the desk when Whitney leaped upon him. He seemed to have no interest any longer in Whitney; as a matter of fact, he seemed to have forgotten him.

"I could be a burglar," said Whitney, hearing, in utter surprise, how his own voice was the first to break the silence. And he thought of the early morning hours when, so uncertain as to how to handle Mogens, he had told himself not to say anything but let his silence work on the fisherman.

Severin did not even look up. From far away Helge's voice seemed to say, "I guess Severin upset me. He called."

"Or someone," said Whitney, speaking very slowly, "trying to get a look at Ørsted's latest notes."

Severin put the papers back into the drawer. "Then, my friend," he said, "you came too late. If you ask me, this apartment was searched before the news of Ørsted's death was made public."

"How do you know?"

Severin shrugged. "I don't," he said. "And I can't prove it. Apparently nothing has been touched, there isn't a sign of anyone's presence anywhere. And as far as I can see, nothing has been taken. Even his papers are all there. But I wouldn't be surprised if they hadn't been carefully copied."

Whitney sat down in the chair opposite the desk. There was a strange feeling of hatred in him toward this man, sitting in Anders' chair with no respect for the dead man's privacy. For a moment he was sharply reminded of Helge standing on the threshold, ordering him out of the room. He wished he could do the same with Severin.

"You speak pretty freely to a man you don't know," he said. "It makes me . . ."

"But I know who you are," Severin interrupted him. "Whitney C. Parker from Jupiter in New Jersey, U.S.A."

Of course—Anders must have told him.

He watched Severin rub mechanically the red marks his thumbs had made when they closed around the other's windpipe, and started to phrase some kind of apology when he caught Severin looking at him, hatred in his eyes. "Your picture is in the paper this morning," Severin said, "with quite a write-up."

Who in the world could have given his picture to the press? And then, as Severin pushed a newspaper across the desk, Whitney saw that the photograph of him was one he had never seen. Someone had taken it, unnoticed by him, yesterday or the day before, for it showed him in the suit he had worn on the trip, his raincoat slung across his right shoulder and his single piece of luggage in his left hand.

"The Danes are a courteous people," he said, reading rapidly what it said about him, noting with relief that his special field, explosives, was not mentioned. "I don't rate this honor."

"Apparently you do," said Severin, and it sounded bitter, "otherwise Anders would not have called you in. Oh, I don't mind. I don't mind." He tapped his fingers against each other with a quick, nervous gesture. "Except I think he might have mentioned it to me himself. I hate to feel like a fool, wake up and see the news of your arrival without even knowing he thought I wasn't good enough."

Severin's grudge and confusion and disappointment burst forth like elements suddenly released.

"I've got the key to his apartment. I go and come here at will. We sat up night after night, not just talking shop, but personally. He made me feel warm, welcome, trusted, as though I were a close friend; then, behind my back . . ."

Yes, thought Whitney, that was how Anders could make people feel, warm and welcome and trusted and then, with a start, he realized that Anders hadn't trusted Otto Severin enough to mention his, Whitney's, coming. He could understand, after his talk with Mogens, why Anders wanted Ulla Rasmussen to believe that he was coming to Denmark merely as a visitor, but why had he not even mentioned his coming to this man who was his head chemist, who was allowed to use his apartment at his own convenience, to whom Anders had talked night after night? Or were these lies, designed to cover up his having been caught searching Anders' desk? Severin was still talking, still complaining, but now it no longer sounded convincing to Whitney. He said sharply, "I still want to know why you think anyone broke into this apartment?"

"Project 11, of course," said Severin. "There are other labs beside the Holger Works working to correct the parenteral action and the hypoglycemic effect of insulin. And Ørsted was pretty close to the goal of finally being able to do away with insulin injections altogether and administering the drug in the form of a pill." He laughed softly and sneeringly, the laughter of disillusionment. "Don't tell me Denmark is the only country in the world where there are no spies trying to find out what's going on in the other camp. Well, as I said before, Anders was pretty close to a solution. He told me so. He took last week off to work undisturbed. But there are no notes. Not at Holger's, not at the farm, not here. What's here is old stuff to me, new to others, perhaps, but where are the notes on his latest findings?"

Did Severin really think Whitney had been called in to work with him and Anders on insulin? He wanted to get up, to pace the room, but he controlled himself and remained seated. Or was Severin assuming that Whitney had been told about these experiments to cover up what he was actually searching for? But let Severin think he believed him.

"In certain stages," Whitney said, "Anders would make very few notes. He always claimed he didn't want to tie himself down. As long as he had it in his mind he was free to imagine what he could not find out by experiment or reason."

"Then he'd changed since you saw him last."

Severin rose. He was of average height and underweight. Younger than I, thought Whitney, about a year or two. Just old enough to have been raised in the Hitler Youth.

"Coming?" asked Severin.

Whitney shook his head. "I'd like to look at what you call old stuff. I might not be familiar with it."

Without another word, Severin went out into the

hall. Whitney waited until he had heard the door close before he sat down on the chair Severin had occupied. For about an hour he went through the whole apartment methodically, no longer sustained, however, by the hope that he would find something. What he had told Severin was true: Anders kept a great many items, that another man would have put down, in his head. He could not quite believe that Anders had changed as much as Severin indicated. What did he believe anyhow of what the young German chemist had told him?

He put his elbows on the table and pressed his face against his fists. A few facts stood out clearly. Severin had searched Anders' desk, assuming, perhaps, as Whitney was assuming, that he had a right to do so. He hadn't known anything about Whitney's arrival in Denmark until he read it in the papers—who the hell took my picture anyway? Whitney thought—he was convinced that there were some notes of importance, pretending or believing that they referred to a drug. How could Whitney tell? How could he know if Severin had not heard about Mogens' fantastic catch? He knew that Anders had been working on the farm but did he know on what? Had Severin talked about the experiments in insulin because he was convinced it was insulin that had occupied Anders or because he wanted Whitney to believe there was nothing else of interest? Severin had

66

tried to make him believe in the possibility that the apartment had been searched. Why? Because he himself had stolen the notes?

Whitney pushed back his chair and as he rose a small, white envelope under the table attracted his attention. Hr. Dr. Otto Severin, Holger Chemical Works, Lingby, Denmark. It must have fallen from Severin's pocket when he squirmed under Whitney's grip. The postmark, as usual, showed where it had been mailed. Ribnitz. "Ribnitz," Whitney read aloud.

He closed his eyes and saw the map he had looked at last night in Anders' bedroom at the farm. Ribnitz lay in the Russian Zone of Germany, directly opposite Denmark, a little inland from the coast. The envelope was open. Still Whitney held it in his hand as though it were on fire, threatening to singe his skin.

When before, in history, had there been a time when the man who was not your friend was automatically your enemy, when indifference was no longer possible, compromises no longer could be made, because what half the world possessed meant danger to the other half, when to read another man's mail was no longer an act of indiscretion but justified by the battle for survival?

The envelope was empty.

Ribnitz, thought Whitney again. Perhaps it was

enough to know that Otto Severin, working at Holger's, was receiving mail from someone living in the Russian Zone.

After a futile search of Anders' desk and safe at the Holger Works, Whitney had to face the fact that Anders had left no trace of the explosive for him to discover. With a feeling of despair he came to the conclusion that Anders must have carried it with him the morning he drowned. All the way back from Copenhagen, he tried to decide what there was left for him to do. He would stay on a couple of days more, a week perhaps, to search and search again, and after that go back to the States. Would Helge go with him? Would a few days suffice to awaken her interest in life again or would the depression over her brother's death be so deep that he would be unable to persuade her? If he did not tell her about his love now, he might never have another chance.

In daytime, and particularly during the summer, the living room at the Ørsted farm was delightful. With the French windows opening out onto the flower-filled courtyard, it was more like a well-sheltered terrace than a room in a house.

Whitney came into the living room, expecting to find it empty. To his surprise he found not only Helge sitting on the couch where last night he and Ulla Rasmussen had talked, but another person. A man. A second later he recognized him from the photo he had seen the night before. Frederick Gabel, the doctor.

He was as slender and frail as he had looked in the photograph ten years ago when he was still a student. His small narrow face was pale, like that of a man who gets too little fresh air, and his violet-blue eyes looked tired. Still, it was a young face. Only his blond hair with a tinge of red in it gave any indication of his age. It was thinning at the temples.

Helge did not even bother to introduce him. "Fred thinks it's absurd to suspect murder," she said instead, the moment she saw Whitney. "I've told him, told him everything you said about Mogens and . . ."

Whitney halted his steps. He had not wanted Helge to mention his suspicions to anybody, had taken for granted she would understand that Mogens' revelation had given a solid basis to his fears and keep silent. But how could he resent her frankness with a man who had been one of Ørsted's closest friends?

"I wish I could agree with you," he said, shaking Gabel's exquisitely thin, long-fingered hand. "But unfortunately I don't. Why are you so sure, Dr. Gabel, that I am wrong?"

Gabel pushed his hands into the pockets of his light gray jacket and shook his head, looking at Whitney as a much older man might regard a hysterical boy, the doctor looking at the patient. There was something sad and kind in his glance, in the smile on his full, red mouth.

"I don't know," he said. "Whitney—I may call you Whitney, may I not?—you see, your name has become quite familiar to all of us—in your field of science you may deny the existence of coincidence, in mine I have gradually been taught to accept it. I could give you any amount of examples where, without a particular coincidence, the patient would not have pulled through. Anders," he said, his glance fastening on Whitney, "used to say that all discoveries could somehow be traced back to a coincidence. I can see that you are, that you must be, greatly disturbed by the fact that on the very day of your arrival Ørsted should so unfortunately drown, but you see, Whitney, he had been working night and day since Mogens brought him the container."

He walked away from Whitney and began pacing the room, not like other people paced, taking long steps, stopping abruptly, starting off again. His was a methodical walking in even, well-measured paces and Whitney was reminded of a professor delivering a lecture, walking back and forth on his dais, so well accustomed to its proportions that he never faltered. Dr. Gabel seemed to know this room just as well. He had also apparently known about the container Mogens fished out of the sea.

"I used to tell Anders," Gabel said, "that a body could withstand temporary excesses. Temporary excesses," he repeated. "But you knew Anders. He would never take the rest he needed. He would go from one problem to the next, night after night, smoking endlessly, drinking uncounted cups of coffee, and never allow himself the much needed sleep which would have rejuvenated the functions of the glands. What I am trying to say," he said, turning around, "is, that during the last two years he complained about sudden cramps, particularly in his legs. I warned him. If you keep your body in one position for hours and hours you can't wonder that with a change of position the valves don't react right away. Yes, I believe in the cramp that led to his death."

His voice was smooth, even, a doctor's voice lulling the patient to sleep. "He can't swim," Mogens had said of the doctor, but Gabel made good sense. Whitney knew it all, too—Anders' habits and the way he himself got cramp sometimes on getting up from his desk.

"Anders," he said, "was working on something which I would call top secret."

"An explosive," Frederick Gabel said. "Let's call it by its name—a new and powerful explosive."

And what a fool I am, thought Whitney, to have wondered if Anders trusted him enough to reveal the contents of the container. Of course Gabel was his friend.

"Yes, an explosive," he said. "But Anders was known for his sympathies for America. . . ."

"We share those."

"I know you do but others might not. The communists in this country . . ."

Gabel laughed. Like his voice, his laughter was even and kind and, thought Whitney, objective. "They don't amount to much. Just consider that Denmark was the first country to enact social laws. Since 1891 we have had old age pensions. Since 1814, when in other parts of the world children were used for slave labor, education has been compulsory here. I don't know exactly when, but for years now expectant mothers have been entitled to free examinations and they have a right to free milk. There are public nurses, free of charge, public nurseries for cases where both parents work. . . ."

It sounded proud and was indeed a record of social achievement to be proud of, but Whitney was not impressed by what the other was saying. The man is a dreamer, he thought. He doesn't know what it's all about. Here he lives, a stone's throw away from countries under Russian influence, yet he has no conception of the menace they are to Western civilization. Doesn't he dare think about it because they are so damn close, doesn't he know that in case of armed conflict Denmark is doomed? Or is he really so naïve as to believe that Denmark has a chance with the Russians?

Then sudden impatience made him speak, more sharply than he intended. "Social laws mean nothing to the communists. In the world they plan, they need complete control of production and the power to rule. They will do anything to get this power and an invention of such importance as this explosive might give them a great advantage over the West. What you say does not in the least diminish the possibility that someone tried to steal the container and, when Anders resisted, killed him."

Frederick Gabel looked at him then, long and pensively. His lips opened as though he wanted to speak, then closed again. Whitney had the feeling that he had offended the doctor deeply by suggesting the possibility of crime and espionage in his country. But just when he expected Gabel to break into another lecture on conditions in Denmark, the doctor shrugged. "I have no doubt," he said, "that one day Anders' body will be found and an autopsy will prove he died of drowning."

"But the container," said Whitney. "Why is there no trace of the container?"

"I don't know," said Gabel. "It must be somewhere. He expected to work on it with you."

To work on it with you. Ulla Rasmussen had not known that Anders asked him to come. The doctor had.

73

"Let's wait till Iver gets back," said Gabel. "Iver, as his lawyer, may know what you . . ." He stopped, straightened a little, as though he had heard a sound which had escaped the others. He turned toward the door. A moment later there was a knock and old Niels came into the room, carrying a small silver tray.

"For Frøken Helge," he said, passing the doctor and walking up to the couch where Helge sat motionless. "The postman just brought this. He says to sign, please. It's special delivery."

There are moments in life when everyday events all of a sudden take on a quality of unbearable excitement. Certainly many special delivery letters must have been delivered to the Ørsted house, but this letter, mirrored obliquely in the high polish of the tray, had that quality of the extraordinary. As though it were a magnet of irresistible power, it drew the doctor as well as Whitney from their separate places to Helge. Helge, herself, after having signed the slip and given it back to Niels, sat staring at the letter in front of her without reaching for it. The address was typewritten and it carried Swedish stamps.

"It's from Sweden," said Gabel, and he picked up the letter, glancing closely at it before he handed it to Helge. Helge held it on the open palm of her hand, weighing it as though it were heavy, the expression on

74

her face a mixture of fear and hesitation; then suddenly, with one quick gesture, she ripped it open.

A key clattered to the floor, a small Yale key.

The doctor, Whitney and Helge stared at it, each of them arrested in their last motion, unable, for a second or two, to move. Whitney was the first to bend to retrieve it, the doctor the first to speak. "What does the letter say?" he asked. "Where does the key belong? Who's sending it?"

There were two sheets of paper. One looked like the drawing of a map, the other was a note containing only a few lines.

"It's Anders' writing." Helge's voice had lost all color. "Anders' writing," she whispered again. "July 22nd," she read, and looked up at the two men. "He was alive then. He was still alive then."

Her eyes filled with tears. Whitney saw Gabel lean forward and put his arm around Helge's shoulder and, though he could understand, even feel, the impact of seeing the dead man's writing, some part of his mind and heart remained untouched, refusing to be caught in sentiment. So Mogens, the fisherman, had been right, this part of him thought. Not only had Anders sailed to Sweden, but he was on his way back when he was killed. That was why the boat was found there. But what had Ørsted been doing in Sweden?

Then Helge's voice cut into his thoughts. "I'm all right now, Fred. Yes. I can read it myself. 'Dear Helge,'" she read. "'Give this key and the map to Whitney as soon as you see him.'" She looked up at Whitney, quite automatically handing him the second piece of paper. "It's for you, Whit," she said, and turned the note around. "And that's all it says. That's all there is." She looked helplessly from Whitney to Frederick Gabel. "This means then . . . this can only mean . . ."

"It means undoubtedly that the key belongs to the place where Anders kept the container," said the doctor. His voice sounded high with surprise.

"That's not what I'm talking about," Helge answered sharply. "If Anders felt the need to hide the explosive in Sweden . . . if he wrote this letter yesterday, then Whit is right. Then Anders must have suspected somebody, some danger. Why, otherwise . . . ?"

"Helge, baby, calm yourself. Don't get excited all over again. Don't jump to conclusions like our American friend here." Whitney heard their voices as in a dream, removed from them by the reality of the key and the map in his hand. Though he had told himself that the search he planned for the next few days might lead to some trace, he had almost given up hope of finding anything. Somehow he had been convinced that the German invention and whatever work Ørsted had done on it had vanished with his dead friend. Even when

76

Gabel had mentioned the possibility that Iver Larsen might know something, Whitney had not really believed it; but now, in his hand, there it was: the place, the house and the key to it, where he would find everything.

It was a simple little map like those one finds on letterheads to make it convenient for a visitor to drive to an unknown location. But like everything Anders had ever done, it was drawn with great precision. Three miles from the farm to Helsingør, three more from Helsingør to Helsingborg in Sweden, across The Sound. From the ferry station in Helsingborg, five miles to a place called Viken; after that, one mile north, there came a right turn and one more mile to a house named Frigga.

He only grew aware of the depth of his absorption when he felt Gabel's hand on his arm. "It does seem queer, Whitney, doesn't it? This business of the letter written yesterday, apparently just a little while before he drowned. I wonder if you or I or, better still, the two of us should not call the police?"

Whitney looked up from the map in his hand at which the doctor was staring with such distress that Whitney felt abruptly ashamed. In his relief that the explosive had been saved he had momentarily forgotten Anders' death. Then the meaning of what the other had said washed away this disgust with himself. He did not want the police called in now. Not before he got hold of what Anders had left behind and handed it over to the American Embassy in Copenhagen.

"Let's wait and see what we find in Sweden," he said, "before we get in touch with the authorities."

American Embassy, he thought again. Yes. It seemed too great a risk to keep it for any length of time in this country in which already Ørsted had been killed. A special plane might fly it to the States, to safety. There he could work on it without . . . The deep sounds of a horn cut into his thoughts. The next moment there was a banging of doors hastily opened, carelessly slammed shut, the echo of rapidly approaching steps. A man came running through the courtyard, a tall young man, dark of skin and hair, calling Helge's name as he ran, his voice deep and clear like the sound of a bell.

"The Pied Piper," Anders had described him. "He didn't need a magic flute to lure anyone into his camp, his voice did the trick. He only had to speak to people and they joined the Resistance. He was only a student but he had the kind of authority that made you forget his youth, that quality of passion which sets aflame the hearts of others. I'm proud of his friendship—Iver Larsen."

Almost at once Whitney could see the effect the lawyer had on people. The doctor turned away from him, his eyes no longer filled with distress, straightening up as though all problems had suddenly been solved, and Helge's face, as she rose, showed for the first time some semblance of the lovely serenity which had always made it so appealing to Whitney. He noticed, with sudden jealousy, how deep were her trust and confidence in this friend.

For a second Larsen remained standing on the threshold, motionless, his breathing the only sound in the abruptly quiet room, then he stretched out both hands to Helge. "He is alive," he said, "Anders is alive." And now his voice was, indeed, like a bell, a bell ringing out happiness.

Helge never took his hands. Halfway across the room she stopped, stared, then turned around and went over to the windows, where she stood, her face pressed against the small squares of the pane, gazing out at the fields. The doctor gasped, then, like a boy who has momentarily lost his powers of thinking, he began to scratch his head violently.

An immense joy surged through Whitney, making him feel as carefree as though his life had never been burdened by loneliness, the seriousness of duties or the obligations that the future might hold. And what a fool he had been to think of murder, of a planned, vicious purpose in connection with Ørsted's discovery and accident. Undoubtedly Anders, swimming from his boat, had suffered a cramp, had not managed to get back to his boat but had been picked up by some craft which had not been able to return to shore until just now. He began to laugh at himself and his laughter started off the others.

"Didn't I tell you," the doctor said, "that you're crazy?"

"I was right," cried Helge, "last night when I told you . . ." She left her place at the window and came running over to where Whitney stood and threw her arms around him. "You beloved idiot," she said under her breath. "I honestly doubt that you've ever worked. I'm convinced you've spent all your days watching gangster movies."

There was in her eyes the light he remembered and he held her tight, his heart beating in his throat, wishing that Larsen and Gabel would leave; and then, as he looked across at them, to see if perhaps they would not show him this consideration, he saw Iver staring at Helge.

At first he thought he could detect in the other's glance only the sadness Helge's spontaneous embrace must have aroused in the lawyer who, as Whitney knew, had courted Helge for years; then the seriousness of Larsen's face made him let Helge go and he asked what they had failed to ask in their first excitement. "Where is Anders?"

"Yes, where is he?" asked Frederick Gabel.

Helge did not ask, but she left Whitney to step up to Iver. Larsen put his arm around the girl and the way he did it was like someone trying to interfere with a blow.

"I don't know," he said. "I'm afraid my news is not all good. I told you first what I thought mattered most. When I got home a little while ago there was a telephone call. Anders is being held by the Russian Secret Police who claim he is the instigator of a theft. The theft of an explosive from a German factory."

"What utter nonsense." Helge moved away from Iver, her anger for a moment mercifully overshadowing her terror. "Mogens," she said, "let me call Mogens. He fished the thing out of the sea. He—oh, you don't know, Iver, but this is what . . ."

Iver raised his hands and Helge was silent. "Darling," he said, "this is a terribly serious situation. Whatever Mogens found or said, the communists have never accepted witnesses from any capitalistic country. Remember?"

The doctor had grown very pale. "Have you called the State Department?"

Larsen threw up his hands in a gesture of despair. "Last year a Swedish plane was shot down," he said. "All protests led to nothing." He turned to Whitney as if he had interrupted him. "Let me finish, for God's sake. Maybe we have a chance. Because this is what the intermediary said. No case will be brought against Anders if the explosive is returned within twenty-four hours. Otherwise he will have to stand trial."

Beads of perspiration were forming on his round, high forehead. It was obvious that he spoke so slowly, so clearly, only with great effort. The hand with which he was trying to light a cigarette was shaking. Whitney looked away from Larsen's hand at his own. It was doing the same thing. He had not been a fool. His suspicions had not reached out too far. The situation was even worse than he had feared.

"I don't know what to do," said Larsen, and began to pace the room. "As I said before, protests have never netted results. Even a country as powerful as America had great difficulty in freeing Oatis. Yes, I do know about Mogens." He turned to Helge. "Anders told me about his fantastic haul and I know that when Anders found he could not analyze it, he cabled Whitney. But I don't know where he kept the stuff. If we knew, Anders would be with us in twenty-four hours."

"We've been trying to find it all day long," said Helge. "Whitney and I started to search for it last night. It's nowhere to be found. Not in his private safe, not at the factory nor at the bank, nor at his apartment nor in his lab, here. You see, Whitney suspected right away . . ."

Larsen looked at Whitney then, a question seeming to form on his lips. Whitney nodded in answer to the unasked question. "I don't know why," he said. "Perhaps it was just knowing Anders or the way the cable was phrased or that I am not able to believe in coincidences like the doctor."

"I wish I didn't owe you an apology," said Gabel, his voice trembling with helpless rage. "What filthy blackmail. To think of Anders being held as hostage . . ." He broke off, his eyes narrowing suddenly. "But of course," he said, "we must be out of our minds. The letter. We have forgotten the letter and the key. That's where it is, of course. In Sweden. Viken."

"What letter?" asked Larsen, looking from one to the other. "What are you talking about?"

The color came back to Helge's face, the light to her eyes. "Just before you got here," she said, "a letter was delivered, a letter addressed to me but its contents were for Whit. A map and a key. Fred is right. That's where it must be. Let's go. Let's go immediately."

Whitney watched her cross the room, so light on her feet, so graceful, and again he was aware that he was watching her only because he did not want to follow up the thoughts racing through his mind. If, to eliminate all danger of recognition and arrest, the Russians had murdered Anders when they had found that he did not have what they wanted, Whitney might have con-

vinced himself that the explosive was not of prime im
portance. But the Russians had risked scandalizing the
world by kidnapping a man of Anders' reputation and
were holding him under a blatant pretext. The explosive must therefore be even more important than he or
Anders had assumed. And the fact that Anders had not
been able to analyze it was proof that the explosive was
probably unknown. And if it was so important, then the
Russians should never be given . . .

And what right have I to decide? he asked himself,
staring at Helge's outstretched hand. What right have
I to say what is more important, Anders' life or the surrender of the invention? Reason then interfered with
the battle of his heart. Reason said with a thin, cold
voice, the key and the map were sent to you. Anders
wanted you to have them. Not Helge. Not Frederick
Gabel. Not Iver Larsen. Not Ulla Rasmussen. Not Otto
Severin. He wanted you to decide, you, Whitney Parker.

But when Anders mailed the letter, had he known
in what dreadful circumstances he would find himself
a few hours later?

Whitney closed his eyes, closed them because he
could not bear Helge looking at him, the eyes of the
doctor and the lawyer watching his lips. This letter had
been written, as Gabel had said before, apparently only
a little while before Anders was caught. He must therefore have felt himself suddenly in great personal dan-

ger, a danger he thought he might not escape, with just enough time to mail a letter.

"I am sorry, Helge," he said. "Anders sent the map and the key to me. Not to you. I think that Anders therefore left all decisions to me and I am certain he would agree that I cannot surrender, never mind under what pressure, a matter so vitally important to the enemy."

In the silence that followed his words all he saw was Helge, turning away from him, hatred in her eyes.

CHAPTER THREE

For a long time nobody spoke.

Later Whitney could not remember how long this silence had lasted, a silence in which he heard the echo of his own voice like that of a monster, repeating his decision. Then Helge said, looking straight at him as coldly as if nothing he might feel mattered, "I should never have trusted you. I should never have given you the letter. Anders made a mistake in thinking you were his friend."

Somehow the doctor and the lawyer no longer seemed present. Perhaps their terror, their helplessness, their embarrassment in the face of this situation, had robbed them of their personalities. They were like shadows, the doctor sitting in a chair near the empty fireplace, his face cupped in his hands, the lawyer again pacing the wide red-brick floor. But Whitney addressed these shadows as though his words might make them come to life, appealing to their understanding so that they, in turn, might appeal to Helge.

86

"It's not just the future I'm thinking of," he said, "not what may happen if one day all of us are involved in a war with Russia, a war in which this German invention may give the enemy a great advantage. Within a short time Russian scientists, or Germans, who may have worked on this new explosive before it was put on a getaway sub for the Argentine, will have analyzed it. From there to production is only a short step."

"What a world," muttered the doctor, as though he had not heard. "What wickedness. There should be no curtains sealing off one part from the other. Science is free. It should be available to all if we are ever to make this planet free from wars. Don't you see that wars can be prevented and life be made worth-while only by the spread of knowledge, regardless of nationalities and ideologies?"

As before he was ignoring the point Whitney was trying to make. But Iver Larsen stopped pacing. "I don't know," he said, his wide gray eyes troubled, "if I can accept this justification of your decision. It seems to me you are using, as an excuse for your point of view, the very attitude toward individual life which we hate so much in the Russians. Like them you are thinking now in terms of what is good only for the masses. And seen from that angle, Anders' life of course counts for nothing."

Whitney wanted to cry out that nobody valued life

87

more than he, that a democracy could work only if the individual thought of the good of all. He grew pale. He looked at Helge, the sister of the man he was willing to sacrifice. If only she would remember clearly, at this moment, what kind of person her brother was, she would understand that Anders would have acted exactly as he, Whitney, was acting now. But what could the cold war mean to this Danish girl? What had Hitler's war meant at the beginning to the Americans, so far removed from the troubled continent of Europe? It was too much to ask.

She felt his glance and lifted her head. "Whitney," she said, "nothing matters to me but my brother. All the reasons you may be able to give, the justifications you may think up, will never convince me that Anders should die because of some invention or other. It may be important to you, perhaps to the world, that the Russians should have no such advantage over the Western powers, but all that is important to me is that Anders should live."

She spoke calmly, her voice steady, not, as last night, a crying, terrified, hysterical girl. And having stated her position, she turned to Larsen. "Iver," she said, "do you still maintain what you said before, that a protest from the State Department would do no good?"

"Unless a miracle happens."

"And you don't think it will?"

Larsen didn't answer, only shrugged, but the way he lifted and dropped his shoulders told more than words could.

"And if he—if it comes to a trial . . . ?"

"Oh stop it," said Larsen, and swung around to face her. "Stop torturing yourself. You know as well as I what will happen. He will be declared guilty of this theft and shot."

"Then," said Helge, in the same clear, thin voice, "then in reality his best friend would be guilty of his death, not the Russians."

Why was it so hard, so impossible to find the words, the right precise words to explain why he could behave no other way. Whitney sighed. "Like you, like all of us," he said, "I love Anders. I would give my life if it would do any good. But this is something bigger than life, mine or his. It is something . . ."

Gabel rose from his chair. For a moment Whitney thought the doctor would strike him, then Gabel turned away from him, his shoulders stooped, his thinning reddish hair tousled from his restless, helpless, scratching hands.

"Don't say you share our feelings for Anders," he said, his quiet tired voice sounding suddenly authoritative. "Until now I was able to respect, if not to understand, your motives, but when you start to sound false . . ."

Iver Larsen broke in then. He put one hand on the doctor's arm in an attempt to quiet him. "Mr. Parker seems to have a different conception of friendship than we have," he said, and Whitney was singularly aware that this old friend of Ørsted's had degraded him to the rank of foreigner simply by no longer calling him by his first name. "I am not saying that the situation does not constitute a grave problem, does not involve consequences of the deepest concern. I know how important this German invention was to Anders and I am sure he would have defended it with his life. But we must see things as they are. Anders is helpless now, as good as dead, if we don't surrender this damned container. What, do I ask, would be gained by his death? Sooner or later some scientist or other, in the United States or Russia, will invent a new and terrible weapon. We can only prevent the use of these weapons, not their invention. Therefore, to me this German discovery is not as important as it seems to be to Mr. Parker."

"Or to the Russians?"

Larsen suddenly took his hand. "Don't think like a patriot for a moment. Think like a human being."

But all humaneness had died in Whitney. He did not know that he had killed it because he could not bear listening to the language of his heart. He knew only that he must not give in to sentiment, must not be tempted by his friendship for Anders or swayed by his love for Helge or his sympathy for these men who were Ørsted's friends. And all he could think of was: I must get to Viken before they stop me.

Already they knew the place, Helge and the doctor had seen the Swedish postmark, Gabel, looking over his shoulder, might even have spotted the name of the house, the red mark that spelled Frigga. He moved suddenly, stepping past Larsen and into the frame of the wide-open French windows. "Let me think about it," he said. "Let me think about it."

He walked out onto the flagstone path that ran along the yard's perfect square as though, to get away from all arguments, he was going for a stroll between the flower beds. Opposite the living room, the door leading into the hall opened. Ulla Rasmussen stood there, incredibly aged, a little old woman who had lost all purpose in life. Whitney walked up to her, stopped and said, "Ulla. Anders is alive," and waited till the news had penetrated her mind, till she gave a high shrill shriek and rushed past him into the court; and only then, when she had attracted the attention of those in the living room from himself, did he run through the hall, out the door and down the path where he had left his car. As he started the motor he saw Iver Larsen running out of the house, heard Helge's anguished cry, "Stop him, Iver. Stop him."

Whitney never saw the red roofs of Helsingør. The traffic on the road that led along the seashore, by-passing most of the old and lovely town, was heavy, and on the stretch just before the harbor cars stood in long lines waiting to get on the ferry. Danish and Swedish cars with a sprinkling of French and English autos among them were all headed for the half-hour trip to Sweden.

Without hesitation Whitney abandoned his plan to take the car across. He drove past the station, past the monument erected in recognition of the help Sweden had given to Danish refugees, until he reached a small harbor a mile out of town which he had passed earlier this morning on his way to Mogens. Here, among privately owned yachts, lay boats for rent. A few minutes later, he was sitting on the cushioned bench in the rear of a small fast motor craft. For the first time then, looking back at the shore, he relaxed. Nobody, as far as he knew, had followed him.

The crowded narrow beaches, the carefully tended gardens of houses above the car-lined streets, dropped back farther and farther until only the castle of Elsinore stood out, controlling the entrance of the sound as it had for hundreds of years. But today, in the sunshine, the imposing Renaissance building held nothing of the grimness of Hamlet's tragedy, none of its importance as a fort or of the vital part it had played once in the collection of the Sound toll. Yet, remembering these periods of history, Whitney was pulled back sharply into the present in which he was being forced to play a part he had never intended. And now, all by himself, he could no longer suppress the doubts that assailed him.

What right had anybody to decide who was to die, who was to live? What mattered more—a single life or the lives of thousands? Other men had been condemned to ponder this question, to make this decision, to battle their conscience, but to think of others did not help. The gulls wheeling across The Sound, the boat dancing on the choppy waves, their salt spray wetting his face, the fast white sails gliding past him—Whitney was not aware of any of it. He sat like one paralyzed, unable to move, unable to master his thoughts. "We cannot prevent scientists from making new inventions, we can only prevent their being used." "Then his best friend will be guilty of his death." "Don't tell us you love Anders." He could not even remember word by word what they had said, Helge, the lawyer and the doctor, but their voices kept ringing in his mind, their accusations, their reasoning, their devotion to Ørsted. What if Anders had not written the letter in the face of expected danger as Whitney was assuming? Or even if he had counted on death and resigned himself to being killed because he saw no way of escape, how did he feel now that his life could be saved? Was Anders at this moment waiting for his release, convinced that Whitney, knowing where he could find the explosive, would exchange one for the other?

"Here we are."

Whitney looked up, surprised. He had forgotten where he was, forgotten the man he had hired to take him to Sweden. They were entering the harbor of Helsingborg in the backwash of one of the big ferries.

"I am going to make fast over there," the man told him, pointing to a smaller harbor a short distance from the ferry station.

There was no passport control. Whitney, who had not known that this formality had been abolished between Sweden and Denmark the year before, thought with despair that anyone, just as he was doing, could avoid the law by simply anchoring along the coast or pretending to be of Danish nationality. How easy it must have been for any Russian agent to follow Anders.

He walked back to the ferry station. There was no need to pull out the map and look at it again. Already his mind had registered every mark and mile. At the foot of the monumental staircase leading up to the King Oscar II terrace he found a taxi. Not quite twenty minutes later he reached the fishing village of Viken.

Here he dismissed the taxi, telling the driver he would take the bus back, and started to walk. After one mile, he left the road and turned right onto a small path which led through some meager crippled pines and birches toward the dunes. Quite unexpectedly, a few minutes later, he reached his goal.

It was a white house with a thatched roof like the Ørsteds' but small in comparison, and from where he stood it seemed completely isolated. Perhaps it was the loneliness of its location that made Whitney turn instinctively. The path along which he had just come lay deserted under the afternoon sun. Ahead of him no one was to be seen, yet, Whitney told himself, the house might be watched. Whoever had abducted Anders might very well know of his arrival and, in spite of the bargain offered, be afraid that a sample of the explosive might be taken before the delivery of the container. With sudden uneasiness he remembered his photograph in the papers. Had it been published for a purpose other than social news?

He went up the sandy path. And as he neared the entrance he saw the name spelled out in seashells cemented into the first of five steps. "Frigga." The moment he reached the top step, the atmosphere of desolation changed, for from here he could see other roofs between the dunes and suddenly he heard voices. But they were the voices of children playing on the beach in front of the house, of summer guests swimming, of fishermen a little farther to the right, mending their nets. Nobody seemed to notice him, yet any of them might spread the word that he had arrived at the Frigga.

Whitney went around the house once more, quickly now, as though it were of the utmost importance that he should lose no time, inserted the key and entered.

The shuttered and closed windows had kept sun and warmth out of the rooms and for a second he stood, waiting for his eyes to get used to the dimness; then, with the caution of a burglar, avoiding any sound, mind and body aware of the possibility that his visit might be expected, he went through the entire house, the two bedrooms, the kitchen, the bathroom, the living room, the attic, making sure that nobody was hiding behind a door or in a corner.

A doll's house, he thought, when he returned to the living room. It should not have been difficult to find what he was looking for in this confined space. Nothing seemed to be disturbed or touched. Dust had collected on the shiny top of the desk, and a little sand had blown in through the primitive windows which did not close properly, the beds were stripped, the linen neatly folded in a closet. Apparently Anders had never slept here. In the small kitchen no dishes had been used. It looked as clean as if nobody had cooked a meal there for a long time. Even the attic was tidy—long chairs, a beach umbrella, a pair of oars, some fishing tackle, all with the strange air of waiting for the summer guests that had not yet come. Obviously this place was a beach cottage, for rent during the season, and not a steady home. To whom did it belong? Who had rented it to Anders?

For more than an hour Whitney searched every corner of it, every chest and drawer, pushing the books from the shelves, probing the walls of the fireplace, lifting a couple of boards which led into a small, low cellar under the kitchen. Disturbing the neatness everywhere, he searched systematically, dismissing a sudden fear that someone had been here before him. But even if the Frigga had been searched and its tidiness restored, nothing could have been found, otherwise the Russians would not have offered to return Anders in exchange for the container. It had to be here, somewhere, but his tired mind could not think of a spot he hadn't searched. It was then when, at a complete loss, he was gazing about him, that it occurred to him that the container might not be in the house at all. Anders had not only sent him a key but also a map. There was no reason why Anders should not have buried it on the property, somewhere among the dunes. And the exact spot would of course be marked on the map. Like a fool, instead of looking at the drawing, he had wasted time. But there was no mark on the map, not a cross, not a line, not a circle. Only the figures giving the distances between each leg of the trip stood out prominently, each underlined: 3. 3. 3. 5. 1. 1.

Whitney stared at them. The map in his hand began to shake. Suddenly he could see the rows and rows of containers on the shelves in Anders' laboratory, not one bearing the usual label from which their contents could be read, all numbered. Whitney, when they had worked together first, had cursed his friend for this habit which seemed to him time wasting, but Anders had answered, "My father taught it to me. He claimed that it was wiser to let nobody know what stuff one had used in an experiment. Also it makes for carefulness. If you are forced to look up on your charts each time you . . ."

Anders had never hidden the explosive in this house, had used this house only to make whomever he suspected believe that he kept it at the Frigga.

Whitney snapped open his lighter. Within a few seconds the flame had obliterated the fine, precise drawing of the map. A tiny heap of black ashes was all that remained on the table. One thing was clear. Anders had not been willing to surrender the explosive to his enemies even when he saw himself cornered. He had taken, rather, the chance of being killed.

In his agony Whitney seized at this thought, held it, spun it out. For him even more than his friend's life was involved. His decision included the loss of Helge. But he did not allow his mind to linger over the memory of the hatred in her eyes, her cold voice, her cruel words. Anders, he thought again. I thought I knew you and now I find I know nothing of you. Nothing. In my greatest need I can only generalize. A man can act like a hero, on impulse, he can rise far above himself in a moment of danger but, given time to reflect, he may change his mind. Under torture . . . He pushed the thought away, unable to follow it through, started again, trying to find by reason what Anders Ørsted would want him to do.

Had Anders intended anyone else to share this knowledge, he would never have thought of this device. The name of the place and the house would have been enough. He had drawn the map because it was his only chance to let Whitney know where he could find the container without giving its hiding place away should the letter fall into other hands. But that did not answer his question. Circumstances had changed.

Whitney rose. He walked over to one of the windows, opened it wide, and wind and rain almost tore the shutters from his hand. In his concentration on the search he had not noticed the sudden change in the weather. Now the beach was deserted. Heavy clouds hung low and the waves rolled in, angry and white-crested. He tried to imagine Anders standing at this window, staring out onto the sea, seeing a group of men coming up to the cottage, one or two or three, going to the entrance door to discover a stranger standing between the dunes, and going back to the room to draw the map, to put it in an envelope and perhaps call out to a child, playing in the sand, or a boy fishing at the little wooden pier, to hand him the letter for mailing. Perhaps nothing like this had happened. Perhaps . . .

Whitney had no time to turn. The blow struck him from the back so unexpectedly and with such force that all consciousness immediately left him.

For a long time, after he finally came to, he could not determine where he was. His head was spinning, his jaw hurt and his whole body seemed to move quite independently, up and down, up and down, as if someone were lifting him only to throw him down again, and every time he was tossed back his shoulder blades were struck by something hard and painful. Everything about him was dark.

Gradually his hearing began to function again. There was the steady noise of a motor running. I'm being driven, he thought. I'm in some kind of car, a truck . . . going where? The moment he heard the splash of water he smelled it, too, and with the smell of water came the smell of oil. No. Not a car, he told himself. A boat. Like Anders.

Undoubtedly Anders had been put on a boat to get

him away. Whitney tried to sit up but found he couldn't move. He was jammed into a space between the open hatch that led into the machine room and the wall. Then his eyes grew accustomed to the darkness and he saw that a small glimmer of reddish light shone to his left. And in this glimmer he could make out two sturdy legs in high black boots and, gradually, the figure of a man in an oil slicker with his arms on the wheel. The boat pitched, rolled, and the chain that held the hatch open tore, the hatch slammed shut. Whitney was thrown clear across the space of the tiny wheelhouse and the man at the wheel, without turning, said, "Don't try any funny business. There's nobody here but us two and you wouldn't know how to handle this ship."

He must be dreaming. It seemed impossible that this man should speak with Mogens' voice. Whitney stretched out his hand to brace himself, found that he was grabbing a mattress, and pulled himself up on a bunk. From here he could see the beam of the cutter's headlights playing across the dark, white-crested waves. For a long time he sat, staring into the turbulent water. Last night all his suspicions had been directed against Mogens, this morning he had dismissed them, believed the story he had been told. Now once more this man became untrustworthy. The story itself might be true, true insofar as that Mogens had fished the container out of the sea and sold it to Anders. But what had happened after that?

If only he could think clearly. If only he could sort out the questions shooting through his mind. There was the neck of a bottle sticking out of the pocket of Mogens' coat.

"Let me have a drink," said Whitney.

Mogens turned then, took out the bottle and handed it to Whitney, but remained standing in such a position that, should Whitney use it as a weapon, he would not be taken unawares. The aquavit burned Whitney's throat. He coughed, tried again, swallowed, and felt the drink warming him like sudden fire.

"Don't know," said Mogens, "why I didn't kill you. Felt like killing you, to tell you the truth. Might still kill you." He pocketed the bottle, this time on the other side of his body where Whitney could not reach around so easily.

Kill me because I suspect him, thought Whitney? Afraid of me as he might have been afraid of Anders? Or of a Russian agent? He felt for the gun in his pocket but, of course, it had been taken away.

"Know what they call a guy like you in my country?" said Mogens. "A stinking swine." He spat and the blotch of saliva landed on the part over the wheel. "Swine," he repeated. "If you can save a friend's life and you don't, then you're nothing but a stinking swine."

102

Whitney decided to say nothing and after a while Mogens went on, muttering to himself, "Frøken Helge calls me, calls to tell me that Anders is alive, and then she starts crying so hard she can't speak any more. So I go up to the farm. And there they are, Gabel and Larsen and the old and the young miss, all talking like mad. Couldn't make head or tail of it until Larsen explained. And while they were still discussing what they should do, how they could stop you from handing over the stuff to your people here, I acted. Words never lead to anything, I said to myself. Cleverer people than the doctor and the lawyer have made a mess of things just by talking too much and doing too little."

If Mogens had betrayed Anders to the Russians, then it was a clever move on his part to pretend now that nothing mattered but to save Anders by regaining the explosive.

"This morning," said Mogens, "only this morning I told you I felt badly, like a murderer, and what do you do but try to make one of me? Think I would allow you or anyone to point at me and say, there, if it hadn't been for Mogens . . . ?"

He swung around, facing Whitney. "And you his friend," he said. "He thought you were his friend. Well, if that's friendship for you . . ." He straightened up suddenly and struck Whitney a vicious blow.

There was no doubt about it, Helge was glad that Mogens had acted on his own and taken his boat to Sweden and caught Whitney.

"It was none of your business," she said to Mogens, but the tenseness left her face and she smiled at the fisherman. Whitney, slumped in a corner of the couch, turned his head away from her as though, by not looking at her, it were possible to think that none of this was true. But he could not avoid hearing her voice— a golden voice, he had thought when he heard it first, four years ago.

"Iver and Fred have gone," she said. "They decided that someone had to stop Mr. Parker after all and when they saw the storm coming up they left before it was too late. They must have reached the Frigga a little after you got there. Where is it?"

"Not on him," said Mogens. "I looked him over carefully. I guess it's still at the Frigga. But I couldn't find it. Then I thought it would relieve your mind to bring him back here as quickly as I could, so's you could question him. Don't worry, Frøken Helge. I left Bertel at Viken just in case. . . ."

"Whitney . . ." Helge came across the room. "Whitney," she said again. "You must understand, you simply must understand that to me, to his friends, Anders' life . . ."

He closed his eyes, he pretended not to have heard,

to be passing out. He felt a warm hand closing around his, not Helge's hand, and a second later Ulla Rasmussen's soft low voice said, alarmed, "You hurt him, Mogens."

"I guess I did."

He waited for Helge to say something, to Mogens **or** to him, some small polite word. She remained silent. But Niels was coming into the room now, he could tell by the old man's steps. "Let me help you to bed, Herre Parker. Can you get up?" And braced by the servant, Whitney rose from the couch, crossed the living room and was led into his bedroom.

Everything looked as it had looked last night, the immaculately made bed, the bowl of fruit, the vase filled with pink and blue larkspur, yet it no longer carried the atmosphere of welcome it had possessed a few hours ago in spite of all sadness.

"Should I help you undress? I unpacked the luggage you brought from town this noon."

Whitney looked up at the old man. Yesterday the voice telling him that no visitors were received so late had sounded forbidding enough, now it was unmistakably hostile. How much of all that had been said had Niels overheard? The hostility of an enemy one can ignore or accept as a challenge; the hostility of people one had hoped would like one was hard to take. For a moment Whitney felt lost, felt like reaching out a hand and saying to Niels, "You've known Anders all your life, as a child, as a youth. Tell me what he would want me to do." But all he said in the end was, "No, thanks. I just want to rest a while."

Niels, as though glad he would have to spend no more time with Whitney, withdrew, and Whitney took off his jacket, loosened his tie and went into the bathroom. His shirt was torn, there was some dry blood between his nose and mouth and his upper lip was split. He slapped cold water on his face, thinking grimly that this was what Helge had meant when she had told Mogens it had been none of his business, a mild reproach for having beaten him up but not, as he had thought, for interfering with him.

He reached for the door to go back into his room but he made a mistake—the door he opened led out into a narrow corridor. From there another door seemed to be the back entrance to the house. He might never again have as good an opportunity as this to reach the laboratory unobserved.

The rain had stopped but the wind was still high. Without looking to right or left, Whitney ran across the meadow, past the farm buildings, never stopping until he entered the lab. He did not dare switch on the light but used his lighter, shading it carefully.

It did not take him long. On the third shelf, in the second row, a glass container, looking for all the world as if it contained nothing but a cup full of some white powder, carried the number 333511.

If Anders hadn't been able to analyze the explosive, then Whitney couldn't do it either in a short time. Also it was possible that it required equipment the laboratory did not contain. Under these circumstances he did not want to touch the bottle, disturbing the dust that had gathered around it. There was no less obtrusive, no safer place than here, where Anders had put it. To find it one would have to carry the whole lab away, work for weeks to analyze the contents of the various containers. For a moment Whitney stared at the shelf. For the first time since he had searched for the explosive, he wished that it might have remained unfindable.

He made his way back to the house without anyone's having noticed his absence, and only when he stretched out on his bed did he ask himself why he had not taken full advantage of his chance. He could have gotten away with it, brought it to Copenhagen, delivered it somehow to the American Embassy.

A fit of despair seized him. He crossed his arms behind his head and lay staring up at the deep brown wooden ceiling. He knew then why he had not done the sensible thing. Oh, he could justify it, all right. He could tell himself that, after all, it was Danish property, that Anders had left it in his trust, but deep down he knew that he had left it in the laboratory because some cowardly part of his mind, some sentimental fiber of the heart had stopped him.

The door opened and Ulla Rasmussen, carrying a tray with smørrebrød, came into his room. "I don't think you've eaten anything since early morning."

She put the tray on the round little table next to his bed and seated herself in the chair across from him. Whitney sat up and poured himself a cup of coffee. "Ulla," he said, forcing her grave eyes to meet his. "Ulla. At least we know now that Anders did not mention he had sent for me because he wanted to keep all knowledge that might be dangerous from the people he loved."

"Drink your coffee," she said, "before it gets cold."

Her voice was as impersonal as that of a nurse and the idea occurred to Whitney that Ulla Rasmussen regarded him as temporarily insane. "If you can be honest with yourself," he said, "if you are willing to be objective for a moment, then you must agree with me that Anders did not want to surrender the explosive to the Russians."

"Anders," she said, with sudden temper, "was in many ways a fool. Too generous, too trusting, too idealistic. I regard it as our duty to save him from himself. If what you assume is true, then it was incredibly foolish of him not to let the persons, whoever they may be, take what they were after in the first place, simply let them steal it, instead of risking his life."

She looked at him for the first time since she had sat down with something like kindness. "You, too," she said, "are a fool. Always were. Impractical. In your own country, if somebody holds you up, do you stage a fight? You don't. You give what you have as quickly as you can, pretending not to see who it is that's poking a gun into your back. Single-handed you can't defeat an armed gangster. I'm sorry, Whitney, but I'm glad Mogens overpowered you before you had a chance to get away with it."

From outside came the noise of a fast-driven car. It stopped. A door slammed, voices echoed from the living room across the courtyard. "They've come back," said Ulla, and rose.

Whitney let her go without any further attempt to argue with her. In a few minutes now the battle would start all over again. He needed these few minutes to compose himself. Slowly he finished his coffee and forced himself to eat half a sandwich, but as he got up to put on a clean shirt, he told himself with a heavy heart that he was acting like a prisoner summoned to face his judges.

They were silent when he joined them, Iver Larsen, Frederick Gabel, Helge, Mogens and Ulla Rasmussen, silent with the particular quietness of crushing disappointment combined with almost unbearable tension. And the silence and the tension were directed against him. Whitney felt their animosity like a physical blow. He straightened and as though this small gesture were a signal, Iver Larsen stepped forward.

"We were unable to find it," he said, "but we know that it must be there, and we also know that you know where Anders hid it." He paused, and when he spoke again, he spoke very slowly. "There was a tiny heap of black ashes on the table. You burned the map, didn't you? The map on which the spot where Anders buried the container had been marked."

"I burned the map," said Whitney.

He looked from one to another. None of them, he knew, would come to his defense but he hoped against hope that, unlike earlier this afternoon, the lawyer or the doctor might at least show an inkling of understanding for his action.

"Do you deny that you know where it is?" It was the doctor speaking, his sad tired eyes strangely alive now.

Whitney groped for his lighter and a cigarette. If he denied it they would not believe him. Viken, he thought quite irrelevantly, the Frigga. Why had Anders pretended to have hidden it there? The question had lain dormant in his mind and even now, when something made it come alive again suddenly and enter his consciousness, he did not know why it bothered him when the reason for Ørsted's action seemed so obvious.

"I do not deny it."

If Anders had wanted his enemies to believe that the container was at the Frigga to lead them away from his laboratory, Whitney could do the same thing. He looked at Mogens. Mogens was staring down at his hands. They were forming fists, opening, closing in restless succession.

"From the fact that you burned the map," said Iver Larsen softly, "we can only arrive at the conclusion that you do not intend to share this knowledge with us."

"That is correct." Whitney stubbed out his cigarette. "As I told you earlier, I cannot see that Anders took all these precautions and risked death, if he was willing . . ."

"I just told you that he is a fool." Ulla Rasmussen's voice had lost all softness. Helge took her hand, held it up against her cheek for a fleeting moment, then made a little step in Whitney's direction. "None of us think that, Whitney," she said. "But who can be sure that Anders knows about this bargain?"

Whitney forced himself not to look at her, for her eyes were soft now, and pleading. "The more reason, then . . ."

Larsen interrupted. "The intermediary gave us a limit of twenty-four hours. It was twelve o'clock sharp when I talked to him. It is almost nine o'clock now. Already ten hours have passed. We may not be able to dig up the entire property and find the container in the remaining time unless you help us. You know the Russians. They may go back on their offer, they may think of some means to find it themselves. They are holding Anders. They may be able to make him talk."

Whitney saw Mogens move and now the doctor, with incredible perception and agility, stopped the giant. How much stronger he was than his frailty led one to believe. In Whitney's aching head the last thing the lawyer had just used as an argument gyrated like an enormous Catherine wheel, lighting up the dark, sleeping corners of his mind. The Russians must have offered the deal only because Anders Ørsted would not speak. There was no need for them to offer anything if they had been able to make him reveal the hiding place.

"That's where you make a mistake," Whitney said. "Undoubtedly they have already"—he looked at Helge, stopped, caught his breath and finished—"tried to find out from Anders. I am more than ever convinced that I am justified in refusing to have any part in the surrender of the explosive."

But Helge had understood. Her eyes widened, grew dark with horror. "They may torture him again," said

Larsen. "They may have stopped trying only because they found out that one of us, you, knows where the container is, and think it wiser to return Anders unharmed."

But this Whitney could not believe. Anders would never have mentioned his name. Or would he?

"Helge," he said, "darling, we have to face all possibilities. Anders may not even be alive any more. Their bargain may be no bargain at all. I am not willing to discuss this further until I am satisfied that Anders is alive."

Mogens was looking at him. "That makes sense to me," he said. "That makes a great deal of sense to me, Iver. I remember once during the war when we exchanged spies . . ."

Larsen cut him short. He turned to Whitney. "You've got something there. Yes, I think you're right. We must ask for more time, we must ask for something or other from Anders' own hands that guarantees us that he is alive."

"I would like to talk to the intermediary myself," said Whitney.

"If I can arrange it," said Larsen, "that seems to me a good way. Let me make a telephone call."

He went out of the living room and into the library. A few minutes later he returned. "They will send a man," he said. "He should be here in about an hour."

An hour can seem as long as an eternity. It can hold a man's whole life, from his first conscious memories to the point he has reached at this particular moment, or it can be filled with flashes as unrelated to each other as the pieces of a kaleidoscope that fall into a pattern only by the deft shake of a hand. It can also seem as short as a second because the mind lingers on a certain thought so intently that time, as time, no longer exists.

What this hour of waiting meant to the others, Whitney had no way of telling. Ulla Rasmussen had settled down opposite him, knitting furiously at something that looked like a sweater, her mouth moving constantly as though she were talking, trying to phrase words she didn't dare utter aloud. The doctor was busy phoning in the library. Once in a while he would come back into the living room, look at the clock and withdraw again. "Lucky it's summer and there aren't too many people sick; still, I'd better make another call."

Mogens was sitting on the step which led from the French windows into the courtyard. He never moved, never spoke. He smoked and the smell of his pipe mingled with the odor of the rain-wet soil and the faint scent of lilies.

Larsen had opened the chessboard and set it up at the far end of the room, moving the men around in an imaginary battle until Helge, without saying anything, took a chair opposite him and began to play with him.

At one point or other old Niels wheeled a table into the room with platters of open sandwiches and salads, tiny glasses for the aquavit and an array of beer bottles. Nobody touched any of it.

To Whitney, stretched out in one of the deep, comfortable chairs, this period of waiting seemed as if it would never end; yet, watching the seconds run into minutes on the tall grandfather's clock, as if there weren't time enough to ponder the situation in all its possible consequences, he thought: Time. If only I can gain sufficient time. . . . If only I could get a chance to form some definite picture. . . . If I could find out where they are holding Anders, if . . . He raised his head.

There was no sound telling them that the man had arrived, yet at almost exactly the same moment, as if the front doorbell had already rung, Mogens straightened and rose, Ulla Rasmussen stopped knitting and looked up for the first time, the doctor came back from the study, rubbing his thin, delicate hands in the gesture of washing, Larsen pushed back the table so violently that a king and queen clattered to the floor, and Helge threw back her head defiantly.

The ring came only a minute or so after each of them had instinctively prepared himself to face the person who constituted their only link with Anders. But none of them moved to open the door; again, as though obeying a secret signal, they waited until Niels appeared and questioningly looked at Helge.

"In here, Niels, please."

She had pulled herself up to her full height and she stood tall and straight, the light of the many lamps—who had switched them on?—making her hair shine like pale silver, her face drained of blood, her eyes hard, her chin set.

Otto Severin came into the room. He came in walking fast, like a man unaware that he has reached his destination. He had not taken off his hat, a soft, shapeless felt pushed deep onto his forehead, nor had he given his coat to Niels, but wore it, as though it were still storming outside, with its collar turned up. He was smoking, and the way he kept on smoking was like a loudly spoken insult.

"Severin," said Larsen.

Even when his voice was toneless, it carried. It was perfectly obvious that he had never expected to find Anders Ørsted's first chemist in the role of envoy from the enemy. His light gray eyes as he looked at Severin narrowed so that they looked almost black. He was breathing heavily.

The doctor seemed too stunned to speak. He made a step forward as if he couldn't trust his eyes, then moved back with the shocked expression of someone who finds himself unexpectedly face to face with a black panther.

"That Nazi," shouted Mogens. "I told Anders he was a fool ever to trust a Nazi."

Helge said very quietly, "You make a mistake, Mogens. He is a communist."

"What's the difference?" Mogens' huge frame was shaking with barely controlled rage. Helge held out a restraining hand, a hand that trembled and seemed unsure of its touch, but when she spoke it was Whitney whom she addressed.

"I told you last night, didn't I, Whit? That he was the first to call, the first to inquire . . . ?"

"Project 11," said Whitney, as much to her as to the chemist. "Project 11. I remember."

Severin shrugged. "Frøken Rasmussen has fainted," he said, and lighted a fresh cigarette at the stub of the old one.

Ulla Rasmussen opened her eyes again. "Did I?" she said, and sank back in her chair, crying noiselessly.

"I was told," said Severin, blowing out a cloud of smoke which momentarily veiled his sharp features, "that you wanted me to pass on a message to Ørsted. What is it?"

Whitney thought of the early morning and how he had surprised this man searching Anders' desk, of the empty envelope which had come from Ribnitz, Germany, in the Russian Zone. If he had been more thorough, if he had forced this man to speak, he might . . .

"Where is he?" he asked. "Where are your friends keeping him?"

Severin's eyebrows went up so abruptly that his large rimless glasses slipped forward on his nose. "Mr. Parker," he said, "I'm not here to answer questions."

Larsen spoke with enormous contempt, his narrow, handsome features set in determination. "Severin," he said, "since you are obviously nothing but an errand boy for our enemies, tell them this: we want some definite proof that Anders is alive, a letter in his own writing. Since he won't be able to say what he wants, we don't need to bother about the text. But we are not willing to consider any bargain without this proof. Necessarily this will have to change the time limit given us for the surrender of the container. Let us say that we will turn it over twenty-four hours after a note from Anders is in our possession."

"I will let you know as soon as I am able if this will be possible." Severin took off his glasses, blew on them and wiped them clear with a nicotine-stained thumb. "But of course you understand that the whole deal is off if you are unable to procure the container. We do not think it can be as difficult to locate as you pointed out on the phone."

"It will be found," said Mogens. "Don't worry, it will be found."

For a second then everybody looked at Whitney.

Severin, not unaware that all attention had been drawn away from his person, murmured in his halting, ungrammatical Danish, "I would also like a guarantee that no sample of the explosive will disappear in the meantime."

"I guarantee that." As though she were swearing the most solemn oath, Helge lifted her right hand. "And now, get out."

What had he hoped to gain by seeing the intermediary himself? Had he childishly believed that he would be able to find out from him who had betrayed Ørsted, or the existence of the container?

The others were talking, talking rapidly, breathlessly and excitedly, as though they could find words to express their horror only now when Severin had left and they were no longer physically faced with the fact that he, of all people, should have been involved in Anders' abduction. None of them seemed to have liked him, each for different reasons had apparently warned Anders against letting Severin work for him in such a singularly trusted and important position. But now nobody found the least satisfaction in the proof that in distrusting Severin they had been right. They were profoundly shocked.

"It must have been he, then, who put the Russian agents on to the whole thing," said Frederick Gabel.

"As a scientist . . ." He stopped abruptly. Perhaps, thought Whitney, the doctor remembered what he had said this noon, that science should be available to all.

Had it been Severin? Had Severin, as Iver Larsen now supposed, been planted at the Holger Works from the very beginning, keeping the Russians informed about what was going on in the laboratory, waiting for his big chance to prove his value to the Party? But if Severin had been the instigator of Anders' abduction, then Mogens might indeed have done nothing more than caught the container in his net and brought it to Anders. Or had Mogens and Severin, had the two of them . . . ?

Suddenly it seemed incredible that he should have let Severin go, that none of them should have thought of forcing a confession from him, making him reveal on whose orders he was acting, to whom he had betrayed the man who trusted him, what exactly had happened when Anders was seized and where he was imprisoned.

Whitney crossed the room, and he had almost reached the door when Gabel said with the utmost politeness, "May I ask where you are going?"

"He can't have gone far—Severin, I mean."

Mogens moved then. He moved, Whitney saw, at a tiny gesture from Helge. Now, as this morning in his cabin, he was blocking the door.

Larsen, who had stepped behind the table Niels had wheeled in an hour before and was pouring himself a drink, looked up. "You're not really asking us to believe that you think Severin would say one word more than he has been allowed to say?" He poured a second glass of aquavit and carried it over to where Whitney had stopped. "He would be a dead man if he did," he said. "You know that as well as I."

He lifted his glass and emptied it in one swallow. "I'm sorry, Parker, but I must ask you not to leave this house." He smiled. "You surprised us by bolting this afternoon. We can't afford to let you have another try in Viken."

Whitney stood frozen to the ground. It had never occurred to him that he might be unable to move at will, might be kept prisoner in this house of which he had dreamed for so many years. Silently he looked from one to the other.

"You heard what Helge said," the doctor murmured softly. "She guaranteed that no sample would be taken from the container. It is very embarrassing but, if necessary, we will have to stop you from doing anything that might endanger our chance of having Anders with us once more."

"I did not intend to go to the Frigga," said Whitney. "I . . ."

Mogens was staring at him; lighting his pipe he was

staring at Whitney over the flame of the match. "We do not trust you, Herre Parker." The little flame burned his finger and he let it fall to the floor. "Why not say it in plain language: we do not trust you," he repeated. "You showed us this afternoon that you don't care if your friend lives or dies."

"It's simply that we can't take any chances," Larsen said uneasily. "You must understand. You alone know where Anders hid the container. It's too easy now for you to go back, dig it up, put some of the stuff away and get it to the Embassy. Not that the Russians could ever prove it, not that I would not want you to do it, Whitney, but the danger is that the Russians might use it as a reason to go back on their offer."

Whitney said furiously, "What makes you so sure they will not do it anyhow?"

"At least then I will not feel guilty."

"You will not leave the house until after Anders' note arrives and then we will go with you." Gabel's voice no longer sounded vague or shocked or tired. Damn them, thought Whitney, in a hot flash of anger. What makes them think that I would ever tell them where they could find the explosive. But he realized that Mogens, Larsen and Gabel would combine their strength to prevent his setting foot outside.

"Don't touch him," said Helge sharply.

Nobody had moved, yet she had been right to speak

for the atmosphere seemed suddenly charged with animosity, the kind of animosity that is based on steadily mounting tension, on general strain, on action frustrated into waiting and the awareness that in a matter concerning all of them one was in opposition to what they desired and to the way they could achieve it.

"His word will be enough."

Whitney looked at her hard. Helge met his glance steadily. "I said your word would be enough, Whitney."

"You have it," said Whitney. He went into the little library, slamming the door.

It was a completely round room, bookcases reached from floor to ceiling and its only window was a skylight. A former bread stove had been converted into a fireplace and in front of it stood two high-backed armchairs and a small table. For a while Whitney listened to the voices rising and falling next door; then, as they ebbed into silence, he stared up at the skylight. It would be possible to get away.

He rose and tried the chain which opened and closed it. He was still manipulating the chain when Helge entered.

"You do not think much of giving your word, do you?"

"Not when it is given under pressure."

"Whitney," she said, "there were three against one.

Don't make me regret that a childish sense of fairness made me stop a disgusting fight."

As he turned, he saw that she looked exhausted. Deep circles had formed under her eyes and her hair seemed to have lost its silvery gleam. He was suddenly overwhelmed by a feeling of pity.

"My darling," he said. "Don't you see that there is no reason why I should be unable to move? It is as Larsen said. If the Russians want to they can go back on their offer whether I go to Viken or not."

"Perhaps. But as Larsen said, at least then, if anything goes wrong, we don't have to blame ourselves."

"Perhaps we will feel more guilty for not trying other possibilities, for giving in so easily, for accepting defeat as though there were no other way."

Helge sat down. "Don't try anything, Whit," she said. "Iver and Fred have finally gone but Mogens is sleeping at the house. There are Ulla, Niels, Jytte, the farmhands, and I . . ." She pointed to her bag which bulged slightly with the outline of the gun Mogens had taken away from him and returned to her. "You would not force me to use it, would you, Whit?"

He knelt beside her chair; he took her hand and gently, tenderly, kissed it. She did not withdraw it but when he looked up her eyes were hard and cold, as they had been when he first refused to comply with the demands of the Russian agents.

"Why have you come in here?" he asked.

Helge shrugged and Whitney rose and put his hand under her chin and slowly turned her face till she was forced to meet his eyes. "Shall I tell you why?" he said. "Not because you have begun to understand what I'm going through, trying to make the decision Anders would want me to make if he were in my place, not because you regret the things you have said to me or because you remember what you wrote in some of your letters, but because Ulla or Gabel or Larsen told you to get me into a mood in which my love for you might make me reveal where they can find the container."

She blushed. A deep crimson colored not only her cheeks but rushed along the fine strong column of her neck. "And what would be so wrong about that?"

"Helge," he said, with great seriousness, "it is true that I have never loved any other girl but you. I think I fell in love with you when I first saw your picture in Anders' room in London, only I didn't know it then. But I knew the moment I set eyes on you. Don't think because my love has been deep and steady that you can take advantage of it or that I'd ever use it as a justification for any of my actions."

"Let's forget about love," she said. "I told you nothing matters to me but Anders. That I would do anything, lie, cheat . . . shoot," she said, "if it would help him. Whatever I may have felt for you, Whitney, died the moment I realized that friendship meant nothing to you. Anders was right when he warned me years ago. Scientists have a second brain where other people have their hearts."

Whitney stared at the skylight. The sky had cleared. He could see the stars. "Then perhaps, with no sentiment involved, you can listen to reason."

"I'm not going to listen to you. I promised Iver and Fred not to let you go."

As though she had not spoken, he asked, "Why did Anders rent the Frigga at Viken? Whom did he suspect? When did he start suspecting anyone? Who rented the house to him? These are things I want to find out, things I think I can find out. And Severin—I must see Severin. I want to speak to Mogens' men, Bertel and Kristen. Perhaps they talked. Or Mogens may have. Or Larsen. Or Gabel. Who are their friends? Above all, who are Severin's friends or connections?"

He spoke rapidly, trying to make his voice sound convincing. "If we could find a trace, some trace that . . ."

But Helge interrupted him. "It's no good, Whitney. Someone phoned Iver just a couple of minutes ago. We will have the letter tomorrow morning. At eight o'clock. That means Anders is alive, doesn't it?" A tiny smile of relief came into her eyes and faded. "And how do you think you could find out anything in the little time we have? It's already midnight." She laughed angrily. "No, Whitney, you're not concerned about Anders. You're only concerned about the container and how you might get hold of it."

CHAPTER FOUR

Helge rose, and as she rose her hair came undone and tumbled down over her shoulders and she looked pitifully young and tired and stubborn. Whitney stopped her only when she had reached the door and put her hand on the round, dark knob.

"All right," he said. "I am trying to prevent the explosive from falling into the hands of people I regard as enemies. But I am also trying to find a way to save Anders."

His tone of voice had changed so completely that Helge turned, bewildered. She had never heard him speak that way, coldly determined. It commanded her attention. She came back to her chair and sat down again.

"It doesn't strike you as odd, apparently, that Anders should have thought it wise to rent a house in Sweden," he said. "To me it is most significant. I don't know anything but that he must have had a good reason for doing so. He could have been killed or abducted right here in Denmark. He could have been lured out of this house, out of his lab, from his office, to any spot or restaurant where Russian agents might have overpowered him. But it looks more as if Anders did the luring. He was setting a trap for someone he suspected. If this person was Severin, then Severin is not the errand boy Larsen takes him to be but someone far more important. That's why I must see Severin. If Severin is only a spy passing on information, then I must find out to whom Severin reports. If I can find that person, then perhaps the Russians will not be in a position to insist on their terms. . . ."

"But simply kill Anders."

"No. Exchange man against man, perhaps, instead of the explosive."

Helge did not respond. "Helge," he said, "let me go."

She shook her head in violent denial.

Whitney stepped closer to her. "You can keep me a prisoner here," he said, "for days on end. But you cannot force me to reveal where the container has been buried. Don't think you can make a man speak who has made up his mind to remain silent." As Anders is silent, he thought, as Anders has remained silent until now. "And another thing. I can leave, Helge. You can't keep me here forever. It would be useless. I may not have the explosive myself but at least I know the Russians haven't got it, either."

"Go back to America and let Anders die?"

He didn't answer, and after a long while Helge said in a small, defeated voice, "I loved you once, Whit. I never ate the American candy you sent me. I let it go stale. I kept it just so's I could have something to touch. Later I was jealous of every letter Anders got. We would never have made that trip to the States if I hadn't pestered Daddy day and night that I was homesick for Anders and after that . . . after that . . . when you didn't come, when you never kept your promise to fly over . . . Iver, Fred, other boys, I turned all of them down. I was living for this day, the day when you would finally say, 'There's a girl I have to see,' and drop everything. . . ."

She loves me, he thought. Even though I did not come earlier, she has not stopped loving me. It was the first time since he had arrived that Helge had mentioned any personal feeling for him. But the moment was doomed.

"And now . . . and now"—her voice faltered—"the man I have been waiting for is blackmailing me, and the life of my brother is the price."

For a second they stared at each other, lost in horror. What had become of them? Who had made them behave this way? For it was true. He was blackmailing her.

There was nothing he could say, and because he could

say nothing to refute what he had to do, he held out his arms. Would she understand that the part he was playing was as foreign to him as it was to her, a part that frightened him no less than it frightened her, or frightened him even more for it revealed a side of his character which was as alien to him as if he had been a stranger from some other planet?

For a moment he became the man she had expected, a man in love. And Helge, as though driven by a desperate need for reassurance, came to him. He held her as he had dreamed of holding her, feeling her body close, their hearts beating as one. At first she stood very still, her head bowed so that his chin almost rested on her silvery hair; then she lifted her face, her eyes, searching his, closed, and her lips parted to receive his kiss.

How long their embrace lasted, neither knew. Whitney was the first to remember that time was running out. How easy, how beautifully easy it would be to say, "Helge, beloved, don't worry any longer. The explosive is right here. As soon as we have proof that Anders is alive we will hand it over in exchange for your brother." Gently he let go of her and even then, when she had withdrawn from him and settled back in her chair, he let a few minutes pass to give her time to collect herself.

"If you would only trust me," he said, "if you would

only understand. I swear I'm not thinking now of getting hold of the container."

"My bicycle is in the shed at the left of the house where the garden tools are kept." She wasn't looking at him, she was opening her bag. "Here are the keys to your car. They told me you left it in Helsingør. If you take the short cut, past the fork, you can make it in about twenty minutes. I expect you back by six o'clock in the afternoon at the latest. Ten of the twenty-four hours allotted us will have passed by then."

She rose, went to the door. "I'll see if everybody is asleep. I'll open the back door for you. Wait ten minutes. If I'm not back by then to warn you, go. Pretend you're on your way to your room, just in case. . . ."

She turned. "Whitney," she said, "Whit, take care that nothing happens to you."

Whitney crossed the Strøget, Copenhagen's busiest section. In daylight, the crowds milling in front of the stores, shopping or sightseeing, the heavy traffic, would have made it hard for him to get through quickly as he did now, late at night, with the city asleep. He might then have noticed the difference between this teeming modern part of the city and the one he reached a few minutes later. As it was, he was not aware of any contrast except that here, in the Latin Quarter, the show-

132

cases were not lighted up and the shops, in cellars or on first floors, were small and dingy.

Once a policeman stopped him, walking leisurely up to him. "Know your way, sir?"

"Kejsergade."

"To your right." Saluting, he turned away, and Whitney, watching him disappear, wondered suddenly if the Danish police, like the English, carried no arms.

Seven Kejsergade was a small, narrow, three-story house. Severin's bell was the top one. Whitney rang, waited and rang again. There was no answer. He walked away, across the street, to see if any light showed behind a window. The house lay in complete darkness. He went back to the entrance door and rang again, this time pressing the bell without taking his finger off it. There was, of course, the possibility that Severin was not at home, that he might be spending Saturday night with some acquaintance or in the company of his friends in the Party. But Whitney had decided to get into the house.

After a little while he heard a small noise above him. A window on the first floor was being opened, then a woman's voice called softly into the dark, "Forgotten your key again, Herre Severin?"

There was no need to answer, for almost at once, from behind the door, came the patter of high-heeled slippers on uncarpeted stairs. A moment later the door opened and, afraid that the woman, seeing a stranger, might close it in his face, Whitney quickly put his foot into the small opening, lighted now by a weak bulb.

"I am a friend of Otto Severin's," he said. "I just arrived today. I'm sorry if I disturbed you."

She was an elderly person with thin, graying hair wound around her head and a scarf across her shoulders. She looked at him hesitatingly. "It's late," she said. "I don't know if I should let you in."

From this Whitney guessed that she was the owner of the house and he smiled. "I expected him to put me up," he said. "I don't know what could have happened to him. I called him this morning long distance, to tell him I might get in quite late, and he said it was perfectly all right."

The woman looked at him, her blue eyes narrowing. "There's no phone in this house."

"I called him at the Holger Works."

Her eyes grew kinder again. Apparently the fact that he was familiar with the place where Severin worked, and knew that he would not even take a Saturday off, reassured her. She opened the door wider. "Come on in, then, and try his door. He may be home after all. Sometimes he's so absorbed in his work that you could drop a bomb and he wouldn't know it and then, again,

134

when he can't sleep he takes a pill. Seems a shame to wake him."

Whitney climbed two steep flights. On the third a window stood open and he stopped, automatically making sure that, in case of need, it would serve as a way of escape. The spires of a church cut sharply into the star-spangled sky. According to his map it could only be the Vor Frue Kirke. He had not realized before that the Kejsergade lay a stone's throw away from the student quarter and the university. Suddenly it seemed appropriate that Severin should have chosen to make his home among the young who were immature enough to be confused by political idealism.

Then, from below, he heard a light, immediately stifled cough. It told him that the woman had not gone back to her apartment but was waiting to find out if Severin was in or if the stranger would have to come downstairs again.

Whitney knocked at the door on which a rather dirty visiting card hung askew on a thumbtack. "Otto," he called under his breath, just loud enough for the woman to hear, "it's me. It's Whit."

He had not picked a lock since he was a boy but as he kept knocking on the door, his eyes scrutinized the lock. Quite suddenly the door was opened. Simultaneously he could hear a door, three floors below, close.

"Oh," said Severin, "it's only you."

His voice sounded so obviously relieved that Whitney was startled. Severin still wore the raincoat in which, several hours before, he had appeared on the farm. Its collar was still turned up. Now he stepped aside to let Whitney enter.

It was a small, poorly furnished room. A half-drawn curtain hid the bed in one corner. On a dilapidated chest a spirit stove stood amid the remainders of a meal, a bowl of tiny pink shrimps, a half-eaten hard-boiled egg and a head of lettuce. Books were stacked up in high, uneven piles against the wall. A desk, cluttered with writing utensils, took up most of the narrow floor space. On it lay Severin's soft shapeless felt hat next to an ash tray filled with countless butts.

These surroundings seemed so unfit for a man who undoubtedly was being paid a handsome salary that Whitney glanced about him in surprise. A student's room, that of one who was hard up at that. What did Severin do with his money?

As though Severin were able to read his mind, he said, "I told you that Anders gave me the key to his apartment. That's where I spent most of my time. There, or at the lab. I just sleep here."

"You heard the bell," said Whitney. "Why didn't you answer?"

"I thought it was someone else."

Severin, Whitney saw, was deadly pale. A vein in his left temple was hammering in quick nervous beats. Now he looked up as if he were still not sure who was standing before him. His head was shaking, his teeth were chattering.

Whitney was seized by a cold anger. "What a coward you are."

Severin's voice was hardly audible. "Oh, shut up. If you were in my place you'd be just as unnerved."

In a flash Whitney remembered a scene earlier in this long, long day, the moment when his hands had closed around this man's throat. Then Severin, instead of being frightened or stunned like any other normal man, had reacted with nothing more than irritation. Whitney stared at him, his eyes narrowing. "Who is the man you're working for?"

Severin looked up, then suddenly, like someone gone unexpectedly insane, he rushed over to the window and drew down the blind. "Has anyone seen you come here? Have you been watched? Has anybody followed you to this house?"

His panic did not seem real. He was panting, his lips were trembling, his hands fumbling at the collar of his shirt, almost tearing the tie as he loosened it. What did he think he could gain by pretending to fear someone outside this room?

Whitney grabbed Severin's frail, bony shoulders and

shook him mercilessly. "Stop acting," he said. "It won't do you any good. Stop acting, I tell you."

"You fool," said Severin, as he had said that morning. "I'm not acting. Can't you see what's real and what isn't?"

Some of the old arrogance had returned to his voice but the pupils of his eyes kept moving rapidly like those of a bird unable to focus. "I'm not afraid of you. I'm afraid of them."

Whitney began to shake him again. "Who are they?"

"Who are they?" Severin repeated. "As if we ever know. They are everywhere. Everywhere. I never thought they would find me but they did."

He ducked from under Whitney's hands and moved toward the table. "And when I saw they'd found me I tried to act as if . . ." He shook his head. "I thought I could carry it off but I can't." He unlocked a drawer and took from it a sheet of paper. "Here."

It was the beginning of a letter. "I, Otto Blancke, living under the name of Otto Severin at 7 Kejsergade, Copenhagen, swear herewith that I never had any part in the abduction of Anders Ørsted, that until the evening of July 24th at eight o'clock I was convinced that Dr. Ørsted had suffered a fatal accident. At eight o'clock on said evening my landlady knocked at my door to hand me a note that had been delivered by a child. It informed me that Ørsted, accused of theft and espionage, was being held by the Russian Secret Police (see enclosed message) and ordered me to proceed without delay to his farm to act as an intermediary on his behalf. Precise instructions on the message said . . ."

Whitney stopped reading. How could Severin imagine he would fall for such a naïve alibi? "If you think . . ."

"But it's true."

"Really, Severin, you can't ask me to believe such rot."

"You must believe me." Severin, forgetting all caution or the late hour of the night, was shouting, shouting and hammering with both fists on the table.

Whitney looked at him coldly. "To whom were you writing this, Severin?"

"To Helge, of course."

"Why didn't you tell us about this on the farm?"

"I didn't dare," said Severin. "At that time I didn't know what I was doing. Something just made me behave as I was told to behave."

"The same something that made you come home and compose this little piece of evidence?"

"I came home," said Severin gently, "and wrote this letter because I was going to commit suicide." He pointed to a small green bottle on the table near his hat. "You get tired of being hunted all your life and it was the only way out I could think of."

"But then you thought better of it?"

"If a man is ready to die," said Severin, "all that he has left is the privilege of taking his time about it. You interrupted me, Mr. Parker. Look at this."

He handed Whitney a sheet of white paper. It was typewritten, some of the letters were jumbled, the margin was uneven, just what one would expect such a note to look like, and it gave the instructions which he had seen Severin carry out.

Whitney sat down on one of the stacks of books and lighted a cigarette. He didn't think of offering one to Severin. "Instead of going home, you could have gone to the police once you regained your senses, as you say you did."

"I thought of it," said Severin quietly, "and decided against it."

"Why? Still dream-walking?"

"Because I was afraid they would retaliate."

Something in Severin's voice, some note of real despair, stopped Whitney momentarily from making another sarcastic remark. And as if Severin had only waited for the chance to speak uninterruptedly, he came over to where Whitney sat. "You see," he said, "if I had not . . . if my father were not living in the Russian Zone, I would never have panicked in the first place."

An empty envelope. Ribnitz, Germany. "Your father?"

"My father," repeated Severin. "I'm all he's got. My mother and sister were killed during the raid on Dresden. He thought I had died, too. He was safe, safe in Berlin. Then he heard I was trapped in the Russian Zone. In Ribnitz. And like a fool he came there. He found me and there we were, united after years of separation but under Russian rule. From then on he planned and plotted to get us away, but only I succeeded. They got him. But they never found out about me. He pretended that I'd drowned. And that's why I changed my name from Blancke to Severin."

He got up and started pacing, knocking into a few pieces of furniture as if he were blind. "After a little while I began to feel safe, to feel I could correspond with him. Officially, understand, I was dead. And now they've found out who I am. Gottfried Blancke's son, alive in Denmark, working at the Holger Works. You saw what they wrote on the message: G.B.'s well-being is in your hands. G.B. is of course my father."

He sighed heavily. "Perhaps you have a father you love," he said. "Perhaps you can understand what it means to be responsible for another man's life or death."

"Indeed I can," said Whitney. "At this moment I am or will be responsible for Anders Ørsted's life or death and you are the one who has put me in this damnable position."

Severin drew back; his eyes widened, narrowed, closed. "You don't believe me?"

"No," said Whitney. "I don't. Not one word."

"Without Anders I would not be here now," said Severin. "He made it possible for me to escape. I wrote him. You see, he knew my father and it was Ørsted who advised me how to make my way to freedom. It was he who picked me out of the sea. Do you think I could betray the man who saved my life?"

"Gratitude is not always opportune," said Whitney. "Besides, I cannot understand, in the first place, what you mean by Anders' picking you out of the sea. Thousands of others made their way into the Western Zone by land."

"I tried it several times," said Severin. He straightened a little in unconscious pride. "But my father and I were important to the Reds. They were watching us. On Anders' advice I tried the sea. One dark night I took a kayak, paddling out as far as I could, and when I was certain that I was close to the patrol boats I upset my boat and swam. I swam for a long time and when I had almost given up hope, there was a rowboat and Anders."

"A formula was stolen last year, shortly after you started working for him."

Severin grinned. For a moment he seemed to have forgotten his fears. "Did Larsen tell you that, or Fred Gabel, or Helge, or Ulla Rasmussen?" He shrugged. "They never liked me. They're jealous. They don't like the idea that anybody else is close to Anders."

A phrase came into Whitney's mind, a phrase he had used only this evening. He had been talking to Ulla. "At least we know now why Anders never mentioned the explosive to you, and that he had asked me to come. He tried to keep anything that might be dangerous from those he loved." Although Ulla Rasmussen had known that he was coming to Denmark, she didn't know why. Helge had not known that he was coming at all. But neither had Otto Severin. His fury this morning had seemed too genuine to be an act. But Larsen had known, the doctor, and of course Mogens.

"When did you first hear about the container Mogens caught in his net?"

"I knew nothing about it until I got the message."

"When Anders told you about it, you didn't go and talk to Mogens?"

Severin sat down on his bed. He moved like an old man. "You really don't believe anything I've told you."

"I believe that Anders told you, not about my coming perhaps, but about the explosive. Since it is a German invention, it seems only logical that he should have asked you if you happened to know anything about it.

I believe that you then talked to Mogens, offered him money. . . ."

"What a bad judge of character you are." Now Severin was sneering; again Whitney was disturbed by his crooked, nicotine-stained teeth. "You could offer Mogens the world and he would not take it if he thought it would harm Anders. Some people believe in love, some in money, some in luck. Mogens believes in Anders."

And how can you judge any man? Even a man you have known for years? Until this morning he had seen neither Mogens, the fisherman, nor Otto Severin, the chemist.

"Do you really think I'll be satisfied with this fairy tale?"

"I'm afraid you'll have to be."

"Who sent you the message?"

"I told you, I don't know. My landlady said it was delivered by a little boy."

"What if I were to take you to police headquarters and accuse you of instigating Ørsted's abduction?"

"I couldn't tell them anything different from what I have told you. And that there are communists in this country they know anyhow. According to the Danish constitution, the party is allowed. If they had anything to do with it—which I doubt—they would deny it, and their agents you can never find."

144

"You have no idea who sent you the message?"

"None."

"Who was the man you reported to after you left us?"

"Oh, they're smart. They wouldn't risk giving away as much as a telephone number. I was told to wait for a call at the station in Helsingør. Just as you read in the message."

Even though Severin answered immediately and his voice was steady, something about him had changed. His movements were once more nervous and his eyes were darting. Whitney said nothing but sat quietly, watching fear seize the man again.

"Parker," said Severin after a while, "even if you don't believe me, believe one thing at least. If anyone has seen you come in here, you yourself are in danger. You are an expert on explosives, you also know where the container is. . . ."

Whitney looked up sharply. He remembered the moment when, in the living room on the farm, all eyes had fastened on him. Severin, he thought, however automatically he may have been behaving at the time, had not been too dazed to notice it.

"Don't worry about me," he said icily.

Severin shook his head. "Fool, fool," he whispered. Then his voice rose. "Don't bother to make yourself conspicuous by trying to find out whom I saw, what connections I have with people, what friends I have.

I have none. I was too afraid to get close to anyone . . . and talk. Talk about my father, about myself. Anders knew that, that's why he let me spend so much time in his company. There is no girl. I don't even go shopping by myself. The woman downstairs, my landlady, does all my shopping for me."

"Thanks," said Whitney. It sounded as he had meant it to sound, bitter, ironical. Severin shrugged and drew his coat closer around him as if in need of warmth.

"I'm just telling you this so that you won't waste any time in your search for the man who betrayed Anders."

"I think the man I am looking for is you."

"Prejudice," said Severin, "is blind. If you've made up your mind to believe in circumstantial evidence, there is nothing I can do. But if I were you, I'd be careful. I'd watch every step I take."

"In fact, you wouldn't do anything at all."

"Anders made enemies of some people in the Resistance," said Severin, "men who were members of the Bopa. Maybe you remember that the Bopa, the communist organization, and the Holger Danske to which Anders belonged, worked hand in hand during the war, united for a time in the same pursuit but for different reasons. They did not always see eye to eye."

"Trying to cast suspicion on somebody else?"

Severin flared up then. "I thought you were old

enough to know that innocence is the hardest thing to prove."

The man is either a superb actor or I am the worst fool ever to try to unravel a web of political chicanery, thought Whitney. He looked at Severin who had stretched out on his bed. "What else have you got to say?"

"You haven't lived under terror," said Severin. "I have. I know what they can do and how they do it. You stopped me from committing suicide when I'd finally got myself to the point. Don't be surprised if you find me playing their game from now on. It's either that or death. And I'm afraid of both."

He stopped, then added under his breath, "I have all the admiration for you, all the respect you deserve, but watch your step, Parker, if you care to stay alive."

In the end Whitney slept in Severin's apartment. He slept on the floor after hours of talk had led to nothing. He had tried to confuse Severin, to make him contradict himself, but Severin repeated steadfastly what he had said before. Like a parrot, thought Whitney, that has learned its lesson, and again, changing his mind, no man can withstand such a steady hammering if he isn't speaking the truth. But sometimes the sincerity of truth sounded damnably like the lie needed to protect oneself or one's organization. Finally he slept, like a soldier, deeply and without dreams, secure in the knowledge that the slightest noise would wake him to immediate alertness.

When he woke it was much later than he had planned to start the day, almost eight o'clock. But he didn't mind. He had needed the sleep and not much could be achieved before this hour.

"The bathroom is across the hall," said Severin, "and there is no hot water in summer—saving electricity." He lay on his bed, still wrapped in the old raincoat. From the way he looked, Whitney was certain he had not closed his eyes. As he searched the dark, intelligent features he thought uneasily that when he left now, there would be no way of telling what Severin was going to do or whom he might see. He could not watch him. Larsen and Fred Gabel and Helge must have felt like this when they had wanted to keep him on the farm.

"Good-bye," said Severin, again guessing his thoughts. "Don't worry that I'll put anyone on your trail or report that you're out on your own to find the man responsible for Ørsted's abduction."

Whitney turned. Severin seemed to be his old self again. An ironical smile pulled at the corners of his thin-lipped mouth but the glance of his deep brown eyes was strangely sad.

Enemies, thought Whitney, enemies. Anders had made enemies among the resistance fighters. Somehow it was hard to picture that there were people who hated Anders. Anders had never mentioned difficulties with any of his compatriots during the years of Denmark's occupation. Had he simply not been aware of any animosity or had he disregarded it as unimportant? Or had Severin made it up? And who would know about it? Gabel? Larsen?

As he thought of the two men the face of a third slipped into his mind, or perhaps he had thought of Petersen the ageing passport official unconsciously ever since he had found, in Anders' safe, the photograph of the little group that had fought together so closely.

A telephone call to Kastrup airport told him this was Petersen's Sunday off and that he lived on Hojbroplads, Number 10. It was when he reached the square that Whitney had the feeling of being followed. As he parked his car, a blue sedan pulled up sharply a few yards to his left and when he got out and walked away, a man followed him. A small, blond man with nothing distinguished about him, unobtrusive in looks, manners or the way he was dressed. Nobody, Whitney felt sure, had followed him on his bicycle ride to Helsingør or his drive to Copenhagen on his way to Severin. Was Severin under surveillance? And if they were watching Severin, did that mean they did not trust the head

149

chemist of the Holger Works and that some of Otto Severin's unbelievable story was true?

Pretending to be sightseeing, Whitney walked up to the canal ahead of him. Far away, across a bridge, he could see the palace of Christiansborg with the premises of the Rigsdag, to his right the Gammel Strand. On a Sunday it lay deserted. Only the monument, showing a woman dressed in the traditional headdress and wide skirt, reminded him that the famous fishwives of Copenhagen gathered here in the early morning to sell their husbands' catch. When he looked over his shoulder he saw the man leaning against the Absalon statue, smoking. Whitney went up to him to get a good look at his face.

"That's the stock exchange, isn't it?" he said in English, pointing at the beautiful Renaissance building whose copper roofs shone greenish blue in the sun. "What a marvelous—what an unusual spire."

The man smiled pleasantly but shrugged his shoulders in a gesture of regret. *"Jeg kan ikke forstaa Engelsk."*

He had a round sunburned face, blondish white hair and small blue eyes. His age could have been anything between thirty and forty.

Whitney went back to his car, started the motor and drove away. He had not gone far when he saw the blue sedan following him.

It was an odd feeling to know he was being shad-owed, a feeling so mixed it was not easy to define. It filled him with anger and at the same time with a strange kind of excitement, with curiosity as well as with a sense of disbelief. Who was the man and who had put him on Whitney's trail? Had Helge told Larsen or Gabel and had one of them, guessing that he would see Severin, sent the man to make sure he did not go over to Sweden and the Frigga? Or was he imagining it all?

"Watch your step," Severin had warned him. But how could he believe Severin?

He drove on until he came to the Hotel d'Angleterre where again he parked his car and went into the large sidewalk restaurant, sat down and ordered breakfast. A few tables away the man did the same. When he had finished, Whitney went inside, inquiring at the desk for a room. They were all taken. He came back to the entrance and the man stood there, this time reading a paper. Whitney passed him and hailed a cab, so quickly that the man, who had apparently thought Whitney would go back to his car, lost him.

Ten minutes later Whitney was back at Hojbroplads and entered Number 10, certain that he had thrown off his shadow. A girl, dressed for going out, a picnic basket in one hand, a large open bag in the other, opened the door. "Sorry," she said, "my grandfather is not in. You'll find him on the Langelinie, taking his Sunday morning walk."

As last night, Whitney was surprised by the gullibility of these people, their friendliness, their politeness, their innate desire to be helpful. *"Tusend tak."*

The girl smiled, a little flattered that he should attempt to speak her language, but she answered in perfect English, "That's nothing to thank me for. He always sits on the third bench after the pavilion."

Together they descended the stairs and it suited Whitney, should he be watched, to be seen with a pretty girl, obviously going for an outing to Klampenburg, Copenhagen's Jones Beach. But nobody followed them, not then, not after he had left her to make his way, first by taxi then on foot, along the Promenade, past the English church and the Gefion Fountain. A fresh wind blew as he reached the Langelinie proper, which runs alongside the harbor. For a moment he couldn't resist stopping to look at the many boats and, opposite them, the old citadel. After the Langelinie Pavilion, he counted the benches. A moment later he discovered Petersen, scolding a child that had climbed onto the rock on which Andersen's Little Mermaid sat naked and beautiful.

"Good morning, Mr. Petersen."

The old man turned around and looked at him

blankly. He got up slowly. "I'm afraid you're making a mistake. I don't know you."

"Not really," said Whitney. "But I've heard a lot about you from a friend of mine, Anders Ørsted."

As if Whitney had used a magic word, Petersen smiled at him. "A friend of Anders is a friend of mine." He held out his hand. "What a shame, what a shame," he said, the smile fading from his eyes. "Who would have thought something like this would happen? It doesn't make sense, does it? A man risks his life a thousand times, nothing happens, then he goes for a swim. . . ."

He lifted his hand and rubbed it across his eyes. "*Jo, jo,*" he said. "God's ways are not always easy to follow. But let me tell you something. He was a good man. More than that. He was a hero. I'll never forget the night when the Germans were ready to seize our fleet and it couldn't escape to Sweden because they had sealed the harbor. It was no time for him to turn up because he must have known we were going to blow it up and there would be hell to pay, but there he was, dropped from the skies to warn us of . . ."

"I dropped him several times."

Petersen stepped back a step, then came closer and peered at Whitney. "My name is Parker. Not that you'd know it. Except perhaps that you may remember I came through Kastrup only two days ago, on Friday."

He saw the old man frown sharply and shake his head. Obviously he did not recognize him and didn't want to admit it. "It's funny," said Petersen. "When you get older you start living in the past. I remember perfectly well what happened five or ten years ago, and even better the events of my youth, but if you ask me what I did last week or last month I have to stop to think . . . and then I'm not quite sure."

He took from his coat pocket a paper bag filled with small pieces of dry bread and threw a handful to the gulls. "Parker, eh?" he said. "American?" He frowned. "Friday," he said, "the day it happened . . ." and stopped. "But you never told me you were going to see Ørsted when I questioned you. 'Tourist,' you said —now I remember. 'Just put me down as tourist.'"

Whitney lied then. "I wanted to surprise him," he said, "and I thought if I gave him as a reference, you might check and spoil it for me."

Petersen, to his surprise, shook his head. "Surprise him, eh?" he said. "But he knew you were coming. He told me so himself."

Whitney stared at him in disbelief.

Why should Anders have done so? He took a chance. "Not Ørsted," he said, "that's impossible. Frøken Rasmussen knew but not he." An idea crossed his mind and he swallowed hard. "Are you sure it was Anders?"

154

Petersen, he could see, was not sure at all. He was confused. Like Fred Gabel he scratched his head. "Come to think of it I couldn't swear it was Anders."

"Well, who was it then?"

"I don't know," said Petersen. "But I heard your name before I ever saw it in your passport."

They were walking up the mole now, between the free and the outer harbor. An English man-of-war lay anchored there, open for sightseeing, and people were streaming up the gangplank.

"You must have got it mixed up," said Whitney. "Perhaps Anders mentioned my name after the war, when it was all over, just reminiscing."

"No," said Petersen. "No. That wasn't it." His mouth was working. He was uneasy. In spite of the little mark he had made on his list he had forgotten what it was that had bothered him about the American. He tried to change the subject. "How's the girl taking it—his sister, I mean? I wrote her a note only yesterday."

Whitney had trouble registering what Petersen had just said. With great effort he caught the echo of his question. "It's a terrible shock for her."

"Everyone who knew him will be grieving."

"Everybody who was his friend, that is."

Petersen said with sudden vehemence, "There was nobody who knew Anders who didn't worship him."

"I understand there are a few who didn't care for

him at all, that he had trouble with some people in the Resistance."

Petersen made no attempt to deny it, but shrugged. "I didn't think you meant those fools who are prejudiced just because a man is born rich. You can't change human nature. Sure, there were quite a few who envied him. He had everything, a famous name, money, and then even authority. They never realized that Anders wasn't given his position because of his money but because he simply was the right man. They thought if their fathers had been rich enough to send them to study in the States, they would have had the ear of the Allies, too."

The old man spoke angrily, as angrily as if Whitney were doubting Ørsted's merits and he had to defend him. Whitney thought of Anders' room in a small hotel near the British Museum, of their many talks and how Anders had never mentioned the animosity of some of his compatriots. How like Anders to take for granted that even war would not alter people's personal or imagined grudges. He wanted to interrupt Petersen, then thought it better to let him talk on.

"And of course," said Petersen, "they resented that he was away most of the time while they stayed here, taking what they called the brunt of it all. They never figured that London wasn't the safest place in the world. I guess they thought of Anders sitting in a club, drinking, enjoying life and only coming over here with orders when he was in the mood, and then just going back to report on them and conditions, as if our own Freedom Council didn't know what it was doing."

Whitney stared across the harbor at the different flags of the ships, at the small kayaks flitting across the water. Perhaps, recalling what had happened ten years ago, Petersen might recall the names of men who had disliked Anders.

"At least," Petersen said, "the boys from the Bopa made it look that way. They played on it. It was with some from their ranks that Anders had bitter clashes."

Severin had not made it up. Severin had not lied. Severin's information was correct. Anders must have talked to the German chemist at length about his experiences. Why should he have mentioned it after so many years unless . . . unless he suspected some kind of trouble from his former enemies. Or had Severin given him this piece of information, knowing it, not through Anders, but from party members, to set a trap for him?

"But you don't remember any particular name?"

Petersen grinned, and the sheepish little grin on the old man's face made Whitney suddenly picture the youth Petersen must once have been. "Human nature being what it is," Petersen said, "we tend to forget unpleasantness. No, I don't recall the names except, of course, for one, one of our famous men who's been a communist as long as I can remember. Professor Mesters."

The name meant nothing to Whitney.

Petersen looked startled. "You've never heard of him?" he said, and it sounded a little contemptuous, as though Whitney were someone from the backwoods. "But he's known all over the world as a specialist on diabetes and a fierce Red. He's been a member of the Party since he could write his name. Many people think of him as a great hero because he was so essential in organizing the Resistance here. Most of the sabotage was planned by him. He got the student body together and inspired them. Anders and he never got along. It's a long story. Years ago old Mr. Ørsted called him a fool openly and Mesters never forgave him. Now young Ørsted comes along and tells him he doesn't trust the communists and he's damned if he'll take any orders from the Bopa. Collaborate, yes, but no orders the Allies would not approve. You should have seen the fireworks."

Mesters, thought Whitney. Professor Mesters.

It seemed hard to understand that Anders should never have mentioned the name. But perhaps Ørsted had not wanted to reveal to an outsider the interior conflicts of his country. Whitney looked at Petersen.

The old man seemed to have lost years; he looked alive reliving the past. Now, for a while, as they left the Langelinie to walk under the trees of the Promenade, he did not speak and again Whitney did not dare interrupt the train of his thoughts but waited patiently for what else might come to the surface of Petersen's memory.

Suddenly he heard Petersen laugh. "Why, of course," he said. "Fred was one of the Bopa boys. Fred Gabel, I mean."

Whitney caught his breath so sharply, his throat hurt. "You can't mean Dr. Frederick Gabel?"

"The very same."

"But he's a friend of Anders'—was," he corrected himself.

"Became," said Petersen. "When we first met him he was a wild kid. One of Mesters' students. He thought every word Mesters uttered pure gold. You see, sometimes we would be up to fifty men working on some special task, sometimes only three. Well, Fred took part only in those actions which made quite a number of people necessary. He was the only Red among us and we thought he'd been placed there to report on us bourgeois. One night it came to a bad fight between Anders and him. Gabel had ordered some of the Danish police, who protected us, to take part in a sabotage action and Anders was against it. He was afraid that if

159

any members of the Danish police were caught, the whole force might be replaced by the Germans." Petersen paused for breath.

"Anders was right, of course. The Germans carried two thousand of our constables to Germany, to a concentration camp—Dachau—and four or five thousand had to go underground. That finally convinced Gabel that everything Mesters said was not for the best and he apologized, and so they made up."

Gabel.

Whitney stared at the English church, so serenely surrounded by a quiet moat, but he saw only the high forehead of the doctor, his tired, red-rimmed eyes, heard his quiet, smooth voice evading the point of Whitney's questions but rattling on about social welfare, remembered it rising a little, "Only if science is available to the whole world will we have a chance to prevent wars."

Only someone you trust can fool you. A wife can betray her husband because he loves and believes in her and vice versa. Anders could be betrayed only by a friend, a man he trusted. And still it seemed preposterous.

"You're sure you aren't mixed up—I mean, you remember the name correctly?"

Petersen looked offended. "Of course I do." He made

an odd little gesture, touching his forehead with one finger and knocking sharply. "I remember something else, too," he said, and it sounded almost triumphant. "It just came back to me now. And that's why I made a mark beside your name."

"A mark beside my name?"

"I didn't trust you." Petersen smiled apologetically. "You see, I didn't know you were Anders Ørsted's friend. I thought you belonged to the Mesters group."

Whitney was at a complete loss. "I never even knew the man existed."

"You told me you didn't," said Petersen, "but I had heard your name before, only I couldn't recall when and where. But talking about all this, it suddenly came to me why I thought you were one of these damned Reds. It was Professor Mesters who mentioned your name. He was fetching someone from the airport and when they walked off he stopped and came back and asked a colleague of mine if a Mr. W. C. Parker from the States had already arrived."

You come to a country you don't know. You meet people you have heard about but of whom, actually, you have no correct conception. You take for granted that certain things are facts and never question them because you feel you have no right to do so. You are prepared to accept your friend's word, and Anders' word had thrown a wall of protection around Frederick Gabel. Now there was a breach in this wall.

Gabel had been a communist, a student of Mesters who was known openly to be a party member. Mesters had asked if he, Whitney Parker, had arrived. How did Mesters know that Anders had cabled him to come at once? Gabel, trusted by Anders, had known about the explosive, had known, too, about the cable. Mesters and Gabel. They were still working together. No other explanation was possible. Had he, Whitney, come a day or two earlier, they would have had to change their plans completely. But knowing that he had not yet arrived, they had acted quickly, abducting Anders before he could possibly pass on any knowledge to the American.

Whitney looked up to find himself behind the university. Quite unconsciously his steps had taken him back to the student quarter where Severin lived. Mesters and Gabel. With the knowledge of these names he might be able to force Severin to reveal what he knew about them from Anders or from party members.

The front door of Number 7 Kejsergade stood open. Whitney went up the three flights of stairs and knocked at Severin's door. He knocked and knocked but there was no answer. He went downstairs again and found the landlady watering her plants and said, "I'm afraid something has happened to Otto Severin. Have you got a key to his room? Would you please open up?"

The woman picked a dry leaf off a geranium plant. "Nothing has happened to him," she said. "He left half an hour after you. Suitcase and all. He said he was going on a trip and he wasn't sure when and if he would return."

"He didn't say where he was going?"

The woman shook her head, lifting her watering can, and as Whitney watched the spray of water wet a small potted begonia, he saw, across the street, the round nondescript face of the man who had followed him.

CHAPTER FIVE

Whitney stopped his car at a sign which read that this
was a private lane, no cars allowed. For a moment he
stood perfectly still, singularly aware of the beauty of
this summer day, feeling the wind and the sun, smelling the sharp odor of the pines which here, at Hornbaek, grew close to the shore. Then he walked quickly
up the lane, between small houses, until he came to
the one which carried Gabel's name. When he opened
the gate in the picket fence, a bell tingled and Helge's
blond head appeared at an open window. The next
moment she had climbed through the window and was
running toward him.

"Oh, Whit," she cried, "I didn't think you'd be back
so soon. I thought it was Fred's wife and the children
coming back from the beach." Her eyes were dancing
and she spoke quickly. "Everybody thinks I was a fool
to let you go, that we'd never see you again." She
pressed his arm. "It came. You were up at the farm of

course, and heard. I left word with Ulla for you, in case you called, and also where to find me."

"What came?"

He had not stopped at the Ørsted farm but had come straight to Hornbaek, to the doctor's summer house.

"Why the letter," she said. "Have you forgotten about Anders' letter? It was delivered at eight o'clock, as promised. I didn't sleep all night. I kept thinking of what you'd said, horrified by the idea that you might be right and it might never come."

She pulled a gray sheet of paper from the pocket of her dress and there it was, Anders' neat, monkish writing. "Dear Helge," it read. "Until now I have been very well. I trust you will make it possible for us to be together soon. Your brother, Anders Ørsted."

Whitney read it twice. "I trust you will make it possible . . ." No mention of him, not a word saying that he hoped Whitney would make it possible. But then Anders, writing undoubtedly under duress, would have avoided mentioning anything that might reveal that only Whitney knew where the explosive was hidden. He was not the man to endanger a friend. Yet the term "you" might include him, too.

"I feel as if I had been born again," Helge said. She picked a daisy from one of the neat flower beds, stuck it in her hair and danced a few steps ahead of him. "As if I had never known that life could be so beautiful.

165

Oh Whit, darling, Anders will be with us tomorrow morning and then you and I . . ."

"Has Gabel gone to the beach, too?"

"No. We went for a walk earlier. He doesn't swim, you know, so only I went in. Never was the water so beautiful." She stopped and said, "Shall we go directly to Viken?"

He didn't look at her. "If you remember correctly, I promised to be back only at six. We have until tomorrow morning at eight before we must deliver the container."

"I remember," she answered, and her voice changed. "But Iver as well as Fred said you were absolutely crazy to hope you could find out anything, that you couldn't possibly . . ."

"I think I did."

Helge's eyes widened. He shook his head to her silent question. "I want to talk to Gabel."

Ever since he had left Severin's room, driven to Hellerup, where Mesters lived in one of the new modern villas, only to hear that the professor was spending July and August in his summer house in Gilleleje, Whitney had wondered what he would say to the doctor when he finally faced him. He had turned over in his mind all sorts of approaches, discarded them, tried again and again only to come to the result that the moment itself would give him the right words.

"He's in the living room."

Whitney walked past her. "Why Whit," she said, "don't you want me to come with you?"

Whitney turned around. She was wearing a sundress, cut low and short. Her straight shoulders were tanned an even brown, her golden hair hung in two thick braids down her back; the heelless slippers made her seem less tall and lent a childish inelegance to her legs. She looked frighteningly young and innocent and happy. He stifled the impulse to take her in his arms and pour out the words of love that were surging through his consciousness. Yet, in the end he knew he could not keep his suspicions from her, and she would have to know.

"Yes," he said, shutting off the desire to forget all their problems. "You might as well hear it."

The living room was a small square, sparsely furnished room and in one corner, near a white-tiled stove, Frederick Gabel sat reading a medical journal. For a moment, looking at him, it seemed to Whitney a dreadful thing to accuse one of Anders' closest friends of having played a part in the whole terrible plot.

Gabel closed the magazine, a thin welcoming smile pulling at his mouth. "I heard your voice," he said. "I'm glad to see you back. I was a little worried about you. . . ."

Obviously the doctor meant that he might have

167

broken his promise and gone back to Viken and the Frigga. "Worried? Were you really," Whitney said, "in spite of the man you had trail me?"

Gabel took off his glasses and put them on again. He looked at Whitney as though he were speaking an unknown language. "What man? What are you talking about?"

"He must be right around here somewhere." Whitney walked to one of the windows and peered out. "He's been following me ever since I left Severin and he stopped his car when I stopped mine at your lane."

"You have been followed?"

Whitney paid no attention to Helge's whisper. He was watching the doctor.

"Are you implying that I engaged a man to watch you because I doubted you would keep your word?"

"I am implying that ever since Anders told you about the explosive you had him shadowed in order to take the container from him . . . that you are working in the interests of Russia."

Gabel sat down as though a sudden weakness had seized him. All blood left his face. "You are crazy," he said. "You are out of your mind. You can't actually think that I . . ."

What else could he possibly answer? Time, thought Whitney. If only I had enough time to handle this with more subtlety. But there is no time. I have to use the blunt approach to get an inkling of the truth from his reaction.

He saw Helge's face, as white as the doctor's. Oh my darling, he thought fleetingly, why must I be the one to destroy your confidence in people? Why must I be instrumental in hurting you?

Gabel was speaking again, speaking with a slow, startled voice. "But it is impossible that you . . ." Again words seemed to fail him. He made a vague little gesture with his hands, pushing at the air as though he wanted to push away the whole dreadful situation.

"You were a member of the Communist Party," Whitney said into the silence.

Gabel looked at him dumbfounded. "Is that what you base your suspicions on? That was years ago. Years."

"Which does not prove that you are not still in sympathy with them."

"Will you let Fred finish?" Helge swung around. "You can't attack a friend of ours without giving him a chance to answer."

Gabel smiled faintly, as though Helge's intervention had restored some semblance of sanity to the situation. "I was nothing but a boy then," he said, "a stupid boy. I didn't know what it was all about. I was young and naïve and impressionable. In those days anything could impress me."

His voice was no longer faltering but rapid and sure.

169

"I was born on a tiny island; my father was a lighthouse guard. Until I was sixteen I saw nothing of life. We were so isolated. All I had was books. And I wanted to become a doctor. I thought medicine could cure all ills."

Gabel, Whitney knew, wasn't really speaking to him; he was addressing Helge, trying to convince her that she could go on trusting him.

"I finally managed to get to Copenhagen. I had gone to a free public school, not a very good one at that. I had no friends in Copenhagen. I knew nobody. I also didn't know my way around or how things were done. In my naïveté I simply rang Professor Mesters' bell one fine Sunday afternoon and told him I would like to be one of his students. From that moment on he took me in hand, eased all ways for me. That was 1941. In '43 we quarreled. That was the end of our friendship and I left the Party."

He spoke quietly and with a great deal of dignity, but suddenly his voice rose. "I find it disgusting," he said, "to have to explain to a foreigner things which are none of his business. That I don't throw you out of the house is due to the fact that I think your own terrible problem has momentarily beclouded your mind."

How would I behave, Whitney asked himself, if I were the accused? He sighed. "Dr. Gabel," he said, and felt Helge's hand on his arm, heard her voice, "Stop it,

Whitney, stop it," and went on as though she had not spoken, as though nothing the doctor had said had made any impression on him, "when did you last see Professor Mesters?"

His question, he saw, stunned Gabel. Some of his earlier vagueness was apparent again in his voice and gestures. "I don't see him. I just told you I severed all connections with him and the Party. Certainly, sometimes I can't help running into him, at a medical congress, a dinner, a meeting, but I never see him privately."

"Still, Mesters knew I was coming. Anders told only you, Larsen, Mogens and Ulla Rasmussen of my impending arrival. But Mesters inquired at the airport before I got in whether I had already landed. What is your explanation for that?"

"Mesters knew?" Gabel repeated. He sounded horrified and utterly surprised. "How do you expect me to explain that? I can't. I don't know. I have no explanation."

Whitney thought of Mogens and how the fisherman had roared with laughter at his suspicions, of Severin and the way he had reacted, first with panic, then warning Whitney. The doctor's reaction was anger.

"Gabel," said Whitney, "I know I have no means yet to make you confess the part you played in Anders' abduction but I will not rest until I have the proof that you were the one who betrayed him to Mesters, who . . ."

Frederick Gabel rose to his full height. "That is enough," he said. "I think it would be wise if you left my house."

He had found out nothing. Had he really thought he could get the doctor to the point where he would say, "Yes, Parker, even though I left the Party, I am still a communist. I believe that under Russian rule the world will finally know peace. That is why I feel justified in having told them about a powerful new weapon. I went to Mesters and he and I, with the aid of Severin and Mogens . . ." Whitney laughed grimly at himself and heard Helge's voice saying furiously, "Really, Whit, you must be insane."

He had not noticed that she had left Gabel's house with him, that she was walking next to him down the lane, past the small summer homes on either side, among sunburned children, through groups of cyclists. "You are like a man possessed, the way you act."

"I am like a man in a lions' cage who has just been told they aren't tame. Which one will attack first? Only a close friend could have betrayed Anders. Only someone who knew."

"In a moment you'll suspect Iver, too," she said. "I

can't permit you to act this way. I can't have you insulting Anders' best friends. Don't you see how impossible your behavior is? Iver and Fred and Mogens, they have been Anders' friends for years. My friends, too. People I love and trust. Many people were fooled when the Russians joined the Allies and attacked Germany. And Fred was a naïve, uneducated boy, just as he said —taken in. Just as people of greater intelligence and knowledge were taken in."

Whitney did not answer. He went over to where he had parked his car and unlocked the door. "What would you say if I or somebody else accused you of being a traitor?" Helge said. "No, Whit. I'm very angry with you. Please come back with me and apologize."

Whitney slipped behind the steering wheel and started the motor. For a moment Helge stood, not knowing what to do, then she got in. "Where are you going?"

"To Gilleleje," he said. "To see Mesters."

"He won't see you."

"He asked if I had already landed," said Whitney. "I have to find out why he was so interested when I got to Copenhagen. Who told him I was coming?"

They were silent then, each staring ahead onto the road, seeing nothing of the changing landscape through which they were driving, the sun filtering through the forests, so neatly kept that there was not a sign of underbrush, past beaches where people picnicked, past meadows on which cows, chained to a stake, stood peacefully grazing, each in its allotted circle, in and out of small hamlets, past crowded hotels and tiny antique shops. At one crossing Helge leaned forward to look at the mirror over the dashboard, then behind her, to stare out the window. "That blue sedan has been back of us ever since we left Hornbaek."

"I know," he answered. "They're very stupid to use the same car and the same man. I feel like getting out and shaking hands with him."

"You're really being followed. They're afraid you're going to get away with the container." She frowned sharply. "I don't like it. It frightens me."

They had reached Gilleleje. Just outside the village high cliffs were evidence of the steady fight between land and sea. Only a few houses stood far above the water, wooden steps leading up to them through the dunes. The wide long beach was deserted. Yes, thought Whitney, an ideal place to rest. They left the car. "It's the house with the blue roof," he said.

Helge suddenly stood on tiptoe. She kissed him. She took his hand. "What does it matter who betrayed Anders or why Mesters wanted to find out exactly when you arrived? You'll never discover anything to change the situation."

174

She pulled him along with her toward the beach. A few minutes, he thought. Why not?

The beach was uneven. They had to cross a few small dunes on which the grass grew. Two of them made a little hollow. They plunged into it. They stretched out on the clean white hot sand. They looked up into the sky. White clouds sailed above them. They could only hear, not see, the water. A gull cried.

They lay close to each other. For a long long while they said nothing. Then Helge whispered, "If you love me, if you really love me, change your mind. For my sake."

He sat up. He stared ahead of him, toward the house with the blue roof. And as he stared, the front door opened. Two men stepped out, started to descend the long flight of steps. One was using a cane. His white hair moved in the wind like the mane of a horse. The other was very tall. Sunburned. He had black hair.

Whitney caught his breath. For a moment he was unable to speak, he could only point. Helge's glance followed his finger. The two men had reached the bottom of the stairs, were walking along the small path, coming over to the beach. Whitney pushed Helge back so that they were lying down again, their faces almost buried in the sand, looking like two young people in love, removed from the world, interested only in each other. But into the sand Helge whispered, "It can't be. I don't believe it. We must be wrong. Tell me we are wrong."

"We aren't," said Whitney, his voice almost inaudible.

The men had passed without noticing them. They were walking along the beach. And in the quiet Iver Larsen's voice talking to Mesters was unmistakable.

Even though nobody connected with Anders was now outside the circle of suspicion, seeing Iver Larsen with Mesters came as a shock to Whitney. "The Pied Piper," Anders' voice seemed to say in the stillness around them. "He needed no magic flute. He talked to people and they would flock around him. I'm proud of his friendship."

The two men were coming back now. They did not cross the dunes to reach the path from which the steep steps led up to the houses on the cliffs, but walked past them, almost to the point where Whitney had parked his car. There they left the beach. A moment later Whitney saw Larsen raise his hand and wave at a chauffeur-driven car. The car, apparently on its way to meet them, stopped, turned around, and Mesters and Larsen got in.

Whitney looked up at the house with the blue roof. Now he couldn't call on the professor. Mesters had gone. He would have to come back. He looked at his watch. Time, he thought again. If only he had time.

"Whit," said Helge. "I feel ashamed of myself." She had lighted a cigarette and by the way she held it, drew on it, blew out the smoke, he could tell she hardly ever smoked. "It is frightening what your mind will do once suspicion is planted in it. You are no longer able to see things as they are, you see them only as you can fit them into your desperate problem."

Yes, he thought. Once your mind is poisoned . . . "What do you mean?"

"Iver," she said. "Seeing him with Mesters doesn't prove anything. He is a lawyer. He might have had to see him on business. One of his clients might have wanted him to talk to Mesters or he might have needed some information from the professor on behalf of somebody."

"Maybe it doesn't prove anything," said Whitney, "but I don't like the coincidence of meeting him in Mesters' company just today. Don't you see that only Mogens, Frederick Gabel and Larsen knew that Anders asked me to come. One of them must have passed on this piece of information to Mesters."

He took the cigarette away from her, inhaled deeply, and stubbed it out in the sand. Watching him, she shook her head. "Why do you believe that Severin didn't know you were coming?"

"I don't," he said impatiently, "but I can't check up on Severin. He's gone. Why do you believe that Larsen couldn't have told the professor?"

Helge drew up her legs and put her arms around them. "Iver loves me," she said, very quietly. "For a long time now he has wanted me to marry him. I told him how I felt about you, that I had to see you again before I could decide anything."

Can you love a girl and risk her only brother's life? Whitney stared across the sparse dune grass at the sea. It seemed impossible.

"Let's go," he said. "Maybe Larsen called at the farm. Maybe we'll find him at home. I must ask him why he saw Mesters just today."

"I warn you," said Helge, "Iver is not as gentle as Fred."

Whitney didn't answer. Again, as on their way to Gilleleje, they hardly spoke as they drove back to Helsingør. Again the blue sedan was trailing them.

Larsen had not called at the Ørsted farm, and when Whitney asked where he lived, Helge shook her head. "I can't have you suspecting Anders' friends. I can't have you insulting these people who have been loyal and decent men all their lives."

"And I can't surrender the container to the Russians until I have followed every trace that might lead me to the person who instigated Anders' abduction." But

178

deep in his heart he knew that he could achieve nothing unless he stumbled on the traitor by sheer luck—or coincidence, he thought bitterly.

Without a word Helge got back into the car. She came, he knew, not because she understood what drove him but because she was afraid that it would come to a scene between him and Iver Larsen which only her presence might prevent.

It was only six miles from Helsingør to Humlebaek, a fishing village and town of villas. Larsen's was a rather big house in the style of the nineties, high above the road. A red-brick wall enclosed a large garden. An incredibly green lawn stretched between huge old trees. A rose arbor led up to the entrance, covered with yellow, pink and deep red ramblers. The home of a rich man.

"Did he always have money?"

"I think so," said Helge, then understood the deeper meaning of his question and grew pale with anger.

A manservant opened the door. "No. Mr. Larsen had a lunch appointment at Marienlyst," he said. "I don't expect him back before three o'clock."

Across the street, opposite the wrought-iron gate in the brick wall, lay a square of private beach, fenced in by wire. A rather long pier stretched into the water of The Sound. On it a sailboat was made fast and on the boat a man was standing, smoking a pipe and shaking his head. Now, as he heard their voices, he looked up and waved.

Helge, as though relieved to postpone another argument about driving to Marienlyst, turned away from Whitney. "It's Svend," she said. "He takes care of all our boats when we put them in dry-dock for the winter."

The man was coming toward them. "Frøken Helge," he said. "I and my wife . . . I don't know how to express it, but we want you to know how deeply we feel for you." He held out his hand. Helge, blushing, took it, and Whitney saw that it was difficult for her not to reveal to this man that Anders was alive. He came to her assistance, cutting short Svend's condolences.

"That boat there's badly battered, isn't it?" he said.

Svend, obviously relieved from having to make further speeches, nodded gravely, *"Ja, ja.* But when you get caught in a storm . . ." He shrugged. "Mr. Larsen asked me to come and have a look at it but I guess I came at the wrong time. He isn't home."

Whitney stared at the small cruiser, the dinghy slung in davits heavily damaged, at the deck from which whole pieces had been ripped away, at the bow crushed as if another boat had rammed it. Storm, he thought, who had mentioned a storm? Then he remembered: Ulla Rasmussen. Explaining why the telephone at the farm had been disconnected. She had told him that there had been a storm the night before his arrival, the night Anders had been abducted. "Iver," Helge's voice rang in his mind, "he will grieve as we do. He is still in Paris. He'll be home only tomorrow."

"Storm?" said Helge. "When was Iver caught in a storm?"

"Well," said Svend, counting by moving the fingers of his right hand with his left, "three days ago I think it was. He called me on Friday morning. But I was so busy I couldn't come before."

Whitney said nothing. He was watching Helge's face. She had grown very pale and the smile which a second ago had played around her mouth looked like a sad little grimace. He took her arm and, as he led her away from the pier, back to the car, she was leaning against him, bracing herself as though she were unable to walk alone. Still, when they were out of earshot, she said defiantly, "It doesn't mean a thing."

"He lied to you," he said. "He made you believe he was in France when you most needed him."

"Somebody else might have taken his boat out. He might have lent it to some acquaintance."

Whitney did not answer. He made no move to start the car but sat perfectly quiet. With immense surprise he realized that suddenly a part of him refused to believe Iver Larsen could have played a part in the struggle to obtain the explosive, in the kidnapping of

Anders. He had pursued Larsen because he had felt he had to follow up the slightest trace but now, when all of a sudden there was a more solid foundation for his suspicion than seeing Larsen in the company of Mesters, he wanted, like Helge, to deny the possibility.

"Why are we standing here?" said Helge. "Why aren't you driving to Marienlyst?"

He looked at her in surprise. "Do you want me to?"

Her face was set. "This time," she answered, "I have to ask him a few questions."

Marienlyst, on the outskirts of Helsingør, was a big, old-fashioned hotel. They drove through its park in which children played and old ladies sat gossipping on benches, rounded the rondel, watched by groups of people drinking coffee under gaily striped umbrellas, and entered the lobby. "No," said the desk clerk, "I haven't seen Mr. Larsen come in. But then, he might have entered from the promenade or the bar."

The dining room, facing its own private boardwalk, was huge. Quite a few people still lingered over the smørrebrød. Helge walked rapidly through its entire length, stopped the head waiter and was told the same thing. "Sorry, no, I haven't seen Mr. Larsen." She turned left to the gaming room. But the boule table was still covered with a white cloth.

By the grace of the Danish king, Marienlyst was

the only place in the Scandinavian countries where one could gamble. Behind the gaming room lay the bar. On a summer day like this it was completely deserted. Helge stepped out onto the courtyard, looked at the promenade, the bathing beach, and came back. "I can't see him anywhere."

She sat down near a window as though suddenly exhausted. Whitney went in search of a waiter and ordered some coffee before he took his place next to Helge on the small bench. Now, staring through the window, he could see the blue sedan which had followed them, parked three cars away from his own. But he had been mistaken in one respect; they, who-ever they were, were not using the same man. The man leaning against it was younger than the one Whitney had faced at the Absalon statue in Copen-hagen, dark-haired and athletic looking.

Whitney turned away. For the first time then he saw that the bar looked like a tiny replica of Krueger's Park except, of course, that all the animals were stuffed. One of Marienlyst's owners must have been fond of safaris. The walls were hung with lions' heads, snakes hid the joints of walls, big horns crowned the windows. Chairs and benches were covered with the skins of leopards and the ash trays were elephants' toes mounted in silver. A jungle landscape, filled with jungle animals. It fitted strangely his own situation. Mogens, the doctor,

Mesters, Severin and Iver Larsen. All of them could have worked together. Each could have played a part in the plot, each could have acted on his own. Mogens because he wanted money. The doctor because he was a dreamer and an idealist who could not recognize the truth about Russia. Severin because he was under pressure, his father a hostage. Mesters because he was a faithful believer in communism. Iver Larsen . . . Why Iver Larsen?

Whitney could not answer the question. Somehow it seemed strange that of all the people who had been close to Anders, Iver was the only one about whom he could form no clear picture, right or wrong. He had seen him only through Anders' eyes, Whitney told himself, never through his own.

"Whit," said Helge, "Whitney. Mesters will never see you until you have delivered the container. Severin will not reappear either before that. Mogens, if he ever had anything to do with it, will never confess. Fred, if he is still secretly a member of the Party will not dare talk and Iver—what could you possibly find out about Iver in so short a time if he could fool Anders over so many years?"

Whitney bit his lip. He had just thought exactly the same thing. But he was surprised that Helge should suddenly see the situation from his point of view.

At the far end of the bar a man sat at the piano. He

was playing softly. Helge put her hands to her ears as though she could not bear the sweetness of the music; then, straightening up, she let them sink back in her lap. "If you don't change your mind, they will kill Anders."

Suddenly, and it seemed to him that it was the first time since he had been told Ørsted was alive and would be exchanged for the container, Whitney could think clearly. For a moment his mind was no longer clouded by the problem of whether he had the right to sacrifice his friend for the possible good of all, his heart no longer affected by love for the girl next to him, his brain no longer searching frantically for some way out. Suddenly his reason worked coldly, logically.

"They will kill Anders anyhow."

Helge moved away from him. She stared at him, stricken. Her lips began to tremble and for a moment Whitney was not sure if he should go on. But her eyes were questioning him.

"Don't you see?" he said, as gently as he could. "They will have to kill him because they simply can't afford to let him come back to Denmark to start his own investigations. They know that he would never rest until he had uncovered the people in this country who are being paid by Russian agents or the agents themselves. Oh yes, I believe he wrote the letter and I believe they will keep him alive until they have the stuff.

Then they'll say he tried to escape or committed suicide. They'll say anything. They always have."

"Oh God," said Helge, and it sounded as though she were going to burst into tears, but she didn't cry. She looked at Whitney dry-eyed. "I never thought of it that way," she said. "What a fool I was to believe that once they had the explosive they would . . ." She broke off and Whitney took her hand.

"As a matter of fact, they can't afford to have me around either," he said. "Mogens, Larsen, Gabel, if they are innocent, can be intimidated, but I am an American. They can't threaten me as they can threaten citizens of this country. And they know that once it is all over and Anders is dead, I would never give up. I might already know too much."

"You mean," she whispered, "Anders and you are safe only as long as you refuse . . . ?"

"No," he said. "No, Helge darling. We are safe only till tomorrow at eight when the time limit expires. Then they will act. Then they will decide that since they can't get the container they must dispose of me as well as Anders."

It was strange to sit in a quiet bar, listening to a soft sweet tune, and talk about his possible death to the girl he wanted to marry. He lifted his head and as he did so his eyes again fell on the man leaning against the blue sedan. He never knew that in that second he

186

had measured his own potential against the strength of the man outside. The idea came quite suddenly, born of resignation and despair.

"Helge," he said, "Helge," and caught himself and spoke slowly and evenly. "There is a chance, a small chance, and we must take it. It may make possible what I have hoped for all along—to find, through the man who is following us, the person who is in back of it all and, if he is important enough, to exchange him for Anders."

She looked at him. "I don't know what you mean."

"I need your help," he said. "See here, my darling. I just told you I was sure that something will happen to me the moment I am no longer of any use. The question is when. Everything depends on that. Go to them, to all of them, call them, tell Iver, Mogens and Gabel that you know where the container is hidden. That I finally told you. That you finally convinced me I had to reveal it to save Anders. That you know the exact spot but that I am leaving, that I want nothing more to do with the whole thing. Go to Viken with them, start digging a yard away from the left dune, keep digging. . . ."

"And you?"

"I'll be on the farm, packing, pretending to leave. If I'm right, some attack will be made on me as soon as you tell them that you know."

She shook her head. "No."

"It's our only chance, Anders' and mine."

"I can't take it."

"You have to. We can't sit here and just hope everything will turn out all right when it's against all reason that it will." And, he thought, they may try to harm you, too.

"They may kill you." Helge put her arms on the table and buried her head in them. "I can't." She looked up. "Whitney, I love you too much. I didn't know I loved you so much."

"It is almost three o'clock," he said. "Don't come back too early. Give them time."

Suddenly she straightened up. "It isn't there?" she said.

He shook his head. "No. It isn't there. Helge, my darling, don't you understand it is the only chance Anders and I have, the only chance for you and me?"

The moment Helge left the farm, fear sprang up in Whitney. He should never have let her go with men he didn't trust. He stood at the window, looking out into the green, peaceful landscape, seeing nothing. After a while he regained enough control to tell himself that his plan was the only chance, that he was right to risk all it might involve.

He went out on the lawn and at once saw the man.

He was walking in a meadow opposite the house. Just someone out on a Sunday afternoon's stroll. Whitney smiled. If he had been sent to watch him only to make sure he did not get away with the explosive, Whitney had no intention of going into the lab now. Still, at Marienlyst, in the deserted bar, he had written a letter to the American Embassy and, before leaving the hotel, had posted it in the box near the clerk's desk. He went back to the house. Only Ulla Rasmussen had stayed behind.

"I never thought your visit would end this way," she said. "Why be angry with Helge? Can't you understand how deeply she loves Anders, the tie between brother and sister?"

"I can," he said. "That's why I gave in at long last."

"Then why not wait until Anders is home?"

"There's no point in my staying any longer since we can't work together. I'm needed at my plant."

"How can you resent Anders' note? How can you blame a man for wanting to live and trusting his friends to help him?"

It was hard to keep pretending to Ulla Rasmussen. Whitney went to his room. There was hardly anything to pack, but he spent a good half-hour over it before he emerged with his bag and put it in his car which he had left in front of the house. At first he could not see the man, then he discovered him, lying in the grass across the road, stretched out on his stomach, facing the house and him.

Ulla came out then. "Don't go," she said. "Whitney, I must talk to you."

It was still too early for him to leave. Since Helge had called Iver, the doctor and Mogens and left to meet them at the harbor in Hornbaek, only a little more than an hour had passed. He followed Ulla to where some chairs stood in the shade of a beech tree.

"She loves you," said Ulla. "She fell in love with you that summer in America. You are breaking her heart."

This time he let her talk without saying much, just watching the time. There was something sweet about listening to confidences Helge had made to her old friend, something sweet and unreal, like listening to the story of a life which now existed only in one's memories. Another half-hour passed and just when he had decided that the time to leave had come, the telephone rang inside the house. Niels appeared. "It's Herre Larsen asking if Mr. Parker has already left." A moment later Whitney lifted the receiver from where Niels had put it down on the hall table.

"Aren't you in Viken?"

"No," said Larsen. "At the last moment I was delayed, and since Gabel and Mogens went with Helge, I thought my presence wasn't essential." Whitney did not answer and Larsen didn't seem to notice the little pause. He spoke on rapidly, "I'm so glad I managed to catch you. I just wanted to tell you how glad I am you changed your mind."

Apparently Larsen expected no comment. There was a certain warmth in his voice as he said, "It was the only thing you could do. But you shouldn't walk out on us now. You should stay."

"I'm sorry," said Whitney, "I've already made my plane reservation."

"If you'll forgive me," said Larsen, "I think you're being very childish. Don't be too hard on Helge. She was almost in tears when she told me, 'I'll have Anders back but I've lost Whitney.' She just called from Sweden. They've got it. They're all coming here. Won't you change your mind and join us?"

Whitney's heart began to pound. For a second he did not know what to make of Larsen's words. Helge could not have told Larsen what the other had just said. His heart stopped pounding then and he told himself coldly: He stayed behind. He didn't go with them to Viken. He stayed behind so that . . .

"I have to return the car I rented."

"One of us will take care of that if you really decide to go."

"I haven't seen anything of Copenhagen, not even the Tivoli."

"You'll see everything you want if you stay."

"I'll be over in about quarter of an hour."

He hung up. He put his hand to his forehead. It was wet with perspiration. He felt in his pocket. It was empty. He had forgotten that Mogens had disarmed him the night before and returned the gun to Helge. He turned around and saw Ulla standing at the entrance. "I'm so glad," she said, "so glad Iver called and made you change your mind. Let's all have dinner together and"—she smiled—"I hope celebrate."

He drove very slowly, thinking not of Larsen but of Helge. At this moment it seemed as though he had never told her that he loved her. He might never see her again.

The red roofs of Helsingør. This time he saw them and for a moment he stopped the car. The sun shone, the wind blew, it was summer, perhaps the last he would see. But Ulla knew where he had gone and if he disappeared from Larsen's house, Helge would not rest. . . . The American Embassy would have his letter tomorrow. He had told Helge to get in touch with them. Somehow, if he died, his death would involve Larsen. It would not be in vain.

He looked in the mirror over the dashboard. The blue sedan was right behind him but as he stopped his car above the harbor, opposite Larsen's house, it shot past him out of sight.

He opened the gate in the brick wall, he walked beneath the rose arbor and it seemed years since he had seen the big old-fashioned house instead of only a few hours. The entrance was in the back. Whitney rushed up the few wide steps leading to the door, then suddenly stood motionless, like a man who hesitates at the last moment, aware that if he walked away now he might go on living. And as he stood, a voice he had heard before said, "You don't have to ring. The door is open." The man who, leaning against the Absalon statue, had pretended not to speak English, held a gun pointed at him and now as then he was smiling politely.

It was a large room, painted dead white, into which Whitney was led. Rare and beautiful old musical instruments decorated its walls. A baby grand stood at an angle to a window which overlooked the sea. Iver Larsen sat before it, trying one key which seemed to have suffered from the damp. It made a strange, monotonous sound. He rose. "It's all right," he said to the man, and bowed to Whitney. "I'm sorry, Parker."

Two, thought Whitney. And Larsen may also be carrying a gun. "Would you tell me what this means?"

"Just what you expected."

Larsen sat down on the bench before the grand, straddling it, completely at his ease. Behind the door through which he had been ushered, Whitney could hear the man blow his nose. "I did not expect a holdup."

193

"I hope you won't mind if I say I doubt that very much. You see, Parker, Gabel told me you suspected him, and Mesters, because you had found out that Mesters inquired about your arrival. Well, to ease your curiosity, Mesters had nothing to do with all this. Don't blame yourself for not following him up. He just had to pass on word to certain people once you had got here. He didn't know what it was all about."

Whitney, without answering, went over to a side table on which an array of bottles and glasses stood on a large silver tray. "If you prefer," said Larsen, "there is also Scotch. A rarity in this country."

A bottle might serve as a weapon, one of the little Louis XV chairs, light enough to pick up, were heavy enough to smash a window. . . .

"So I was warned," said Larsen. "I knew once you had started to suspect Anders' closest friends that my turn would come."

Whitney, still saying nothing, sat down and lighted a cigarette. Larsen was smiling at him. "Despise me so much that you won't even talk?" Whitney did not answer and after a moment Larsen shrugged. "In America," he said, "you may be able to afford loyalty. Unfortunately I was not born in the States. There is an old saying, how you make your bed so you must lie. Well, if ever it comes to an armed conflict between your country and the Russians, Denmark will be overrun before American planes can appear. I have no confidence in our army, either; that is, I don't think they could hold out until you came to our aid."

There was only one door and in front of that door the man had been posted.

"As a lawyer," said Larsen, "I am not essential to a communistically ruled country. Manual labor or science they can use, but a lawyer is doomed, and since I've learned nothing else . . . I decided to throw in my lot with the power closest to us. That's good sense, isn't it?"

Whitney spoke for the first time. "The events of the last years should have taught you the lesson that everybody is expendable once they have become valueless."

Larsen laughed then. "I intend to keep on being of value. I can play their game, too. Nobody will ever know that I've been working in the interests of Russia for years. To the outside world I'll be a hero. Whenever I turn up in another country I'll be a martyr. A man who managed to get away, was caught, brought back, managed to escape again. . . ."

Whitney got up, started to pace the room, and Larsen said quietly, "I'd rather you wouldn't move about."

Whitney, as though he had not heard, kept walking.

"Don't be a fool," said Larsen, "I have a gun." He shook his head. "You see, you made a mistake in thinking in humane terms. You should never have revealed to Helge where the explosive was hidden. But then you had no chance of getting out of this country with or without it."

"I knew that," said Whitney. "What will happen to Anders?"

"That is out of my hands."

"Helge?"

"Oh, I think I can protect her."

"You think the position you hold is strong enough to see no harm will come to her?"

Larsen smiled, a condescending smile. It told Whitney what he wanted to know.

"What part have Mogens, Severin and the doctor in all this?"

"You are asking questions like a man who is going to live," said Larsen.

Whitney sat down in the chair he had occupied before. "But I expect to live," he said.

Larsen looked up. "Wouldn't you call your hopes a little too optimistic under the circumstances?"

"Not at all," said Whitney. "For you see, Larsen, Helge does not know where the explosive is. Nobody knows except me. But I figured that whoever was responsible for Anders' abduction would act once he thought he had it."

"But Helge called," said Larsen. "Don't think for a moment that I believe you're telling the truth." He got up, however, and now it was he who paced the floor.

"You'll soon find out," said Whitney, and he was out of his chair and over at the side table, grabbing a full bottle and hurling it at Larsen before the other had turned in his direction.

It hit Larsen on the shoulder, then crashed to the floor. Larsen went down and Whitney had lifted a chair and smashed a window before the man posted outside came rushing into the room. But the hole he had made wasn't big enough to escape through and the man was upon him before he had time to swing the chair again. The next moment Larsen pulled himself up from the floor.

Two, thought Whitney, as he had thought before. I have no chance against two. He was tied to the chair, helpless. There he was, Iver Larsen, the man he had hoped to find, the man important enough to be offered in exchange for Anders—and he could do nothing about it.

"You don't really think you'll get away with it?" he said. "There will be inquiries. . . . Helge . . ."

"Don't worry," Larsen told him. "Other people have disappeared and never been found. At six o'clock some-one who looks like you will board the plane for Paris-New York. He will arrive in Paris, decide to stay over, register at some small hotel and never be heard from again. Nothing will have happened to you in this country."

Whitney looked up to see that Larsen was holding his passport in his hand, waving it at him like a small green flag of triumph.

"Except that Helge won't believe I have left."

"There are ways of making her believe what is best for her."

Whitney closed his eyes. Terror seized him and he could no longer think clearly.

CHAPTER SIX

Larsen sat down in front of the grand. He straightened the fold of his trousers before he began to play softly.

"Bach," he said. "There is nothing like Bach for making you forget the world, for helping you to think clearly, for soothing your nerves."

For a while no sound but the music filled the room. Larsen played well and Whitney watched the anger leave his face until it became almost serene. Without stopping, Larsen said over his shoulder, "You should have learned to take things in your stride, Mr. Parker, instead of letting curiosity get the better of you."

Whitney said nothing. A clock could be heard ringing out the hour. Larsen stopped playing. "I'll leave now," he said, "to keep my appointment with Helge and the others at Gabel's house. My man will watch you. Any message for Helge?"

"Tell her . . ." said Whitney, and stopped. From behind the door came a scream, the scream of a man in agony.

It all happened in a moment, yet it seemed an eternity. In that moment Larsen rose, cocked his revolver, a door slammed somewhere, the man who had helped overpower Whitney could be seen running down the garden path holding both hands high over his head in the gesture of surrender, and the door opened. It opened very slowly and Larsen lifted his gun, then let it sink again in utter astonishment. On the threshold stood Helge. She stood very quietly.

"So Whitney was right," she said, "you never were in Paris. You were here all the time, to see that everything went according to plan."

She crossed the room to where Whitney sat tied to his chair, and as Larsen's eyes followed her movements, Mogens rushed into the room. He came in like a bull, his body bent, his head lowered and, like a bull, he rushed at Larsen. A shot went wild and Mogens was on top of Larsen, holding him down, his huge body almost crushing the lawyer.

"Don't kill him," said Whitney, "don't kill him. We need him." And he said it again, for Mogens seemed deaf to the world. Then Helge was untying the ropes that held Whitney helpless.

"You see," she said, "he didn't come. He said he would when I spoke to him from the farm but when I got to Hornbaek he had called Fred to say he couldn't make it. That startled me. All the way over to Viken I

200

wondered why he hadn't come. And then I remembered you had said that as soon as they knew the explosive had been found, they would try to attack you. That's why I called him and lied about finding the container. I could never have done it if you hadn't said that it was all a question of time. You aren't hurt, Whit darling?"

"Go on," he said, and smiled at her.

"That's really all." She bent and kissed him. "I phoned the farm and Ulla said you had gone to his house and I was so afraid that I decided to tell Mogens and Gabel the truth. Gabel would not believe it but Mogens came with me. So we crossed directly from Viken to Humlebaek. We surprised the man but somehow he escaped. Does it matter?"

"No," he said, "I don't think it does."

He got out of the chair and pulled her close. For a moment he held her, in deep amazement that she should have acted so cleverly, so courageously, held her with an immense feeling of happiness, triumphant about the turn things had taken. Then he let go of her and picked up the revolver which had fallen to the floor when Mogens attacked Larsen.

"Now we will see," he said to the lawyer, "how important you are to your friends, and I hope you spoke the truth when you told me you were of great value to them."

He made a sign to Mogens to let Larsen rise. Helge,

he saw, was looking away, trying not to face the man Anders and she had considered their friend.

"What do you intend to do?"

Larsen spoke with his usual easy, suave voice but his face was white and he was biting his lip nervously.

"At all times countries have exchanged people who were important to them," said Whitney, "to avoid a trial during which they might talk. Naturally I will make my report to the authorities and there is no doubt that they will not rest until they have uncovered the people with whom you worked. But instead of handing you over to the police, I am ready to exchange you for Anders."

Larsen did not answer.

"You will phone your people," said Whitney, "and repeat my offer to them." He went over to the side table and poured himself a drink, then filled a glass for Larsen.

Larsen's hand was steady as he took it. Whitney waited till he had finished, then pointed to the telephone on a small table near the door. To his relief Larsen did not hesitate and as he dialed a number, Whitney thought with a feeling of elation; I've found the right man.

Nobody spoke while they waited for the call to come through. Helge was sitting on the bench in front of the piano, her back to Larsen so that Whitney could not see her face, either. Mogens, barring the door an inch or two away from the lawyer, looked strangely like a child, a child that no longer understands anything in life. Whitney started to pace the room. He stopped only when he heard Larsen's voice.

"At this moment Parker is in control of the situation. I'm sorry, but I couldn't do anything about it. He offers, instead of handing me over to the authorities, to exchange me for the person you are holding."

He was silent, then he nodded. "All right. I'll be waiting." He put down the receiver. "They will see if it can be arranged," he said. "They will call back. It may take an hour or two."

Nothing in his face showed what he might be feeling or thinking. "An eye for an eye," said Mogens, "a tooth for a tooth. If they have twisted so much as a hair of Anders' head you'll pay for it."

Larsen paid no attention to the fisherman. "I would like to retire to my study," he said.

The study was a room on the second floor with two windows overlooking the garden. It offered no chance of escape. The distance to the ground was such that anyone trying to jump would be severely injured. Larsen made not the slightest attempt at resistance when Whitney searched the room carefully, then asked Larsen to hand over the keys to his desk. He stood at the open window, staring across the tops of the trees, out to sea.

"You'll find nothing of interest," he said. "I never kept anything here."

Whitney locked the door leading to the bedroom, taking the key with him, then quietly closed the door to the hall behind him, turning the key in that lock, too. "You stay here, Mogens, outside his room."

"You think you know people." Mogens took the gun Whitney was handing him. "I have known him since I was knee high and he only a year or two younger. I taught him how to sail a boat. Taught him how to fish. Taught him one summer how to drink without showing it. We fought side by side during the war. We . . ." He sat down on the staircase, shaking his head.

"I don't want to stay in this house." Helge took Whitney's arm. But she wouldn't hear of his suggestion to go back to the farm and wait there for him. "It's just that I don't want to see him or anything that has to do with him." They were downstairs in the music room again. "So many nights," she whispered, "Anders and I, sitting on the window seat, listening to him playing, so many hours . . . Let's go out in the garden, Whit."

The traffic on the road below had grown a little less heavy. Something of the peace of approaching evening lay over the landscape, the smell of roses seemed heavier, the lawn greener. Only the wind was still high, singing across the sound.

"How late is it?"

204

"Just over an hour."

"Already?" They could not grasp the fact that time was flying. "An hour or two," Larsen had said. The answer might come any moment now.

After a while, the fear of missing the call drove them back to the house. Mogens was sitting just as they had left him, on top of the stairs. "No sound from in there," he said, pointing with his thumb over his shoulder. "Must be asleep, but how a man like him can sleep . . ."

Helge sat down next to him. Whitney remained standing, leaning against the heavy oak balustrade. For the first time now he allowed his mind to linger on the dangers passed. "If you hadn't come," he said, and stopped. It sounded like a shot. Yet it couldn't have been a shot. He had made sure before he closed the door of Larsen's room that there was no second revolver anywhere in the study.

"Must have been a car backfiring," said Mogens, but even as he was saying it, he was running across the hall. Then he stopped, looking at Whitney and Helge who had followed him. Suddenly Whitney's hand shook and it was Mogens, after all, who turned the key.

Larsen lay on the floor near the open window. The bullet had gone through his head. "Don't look," Whitney said to Helge. "Don't, darling." He pushed her back out of the room.

"I thought I searched him." Mogens kneeled down

near the dead man. "He must have had a second gun hidden somewhere." He looked up at Whitney. "But I can't find it. I can't see it anywhere. And it certainly should be right here."

Whitney stepped up to the window. He saw the tree, straight and beautiful and of great height. Its crown reached higher than the second floor and it stood only about forty yards from the house. Below it, on the ground, on the white pebbles, lay something he had not noticed before, a few small branches like those that might break if someone were to climb the tree. They didn't even bother to make it look like suicide, he thought. They shot him. Somebody was sent to shoot him. He wasn't so important after all.

"Don't bother," he said to Mogens. But Mogens had understood. He was standing next to Whitney, staring down at the ground around the tree.

"That's their answer, isn't it, Herre Parker?" he said.

Whitney could only nod. In his disappointment and despair he felt like a small boy, very close to tears.

"You did everything you could." Mogens put his hand on Whitney's shoulder. "You risked your life, knowing you might be killed. We couldn't have prevented it, could we?"

"I don't know," said Whitney. "I don't know. Perhaps I shouldn't have been so sure it would work. If I hadn't been so sure I might have thought of some other way before they killed him. Call the police, Mogens. I think we can no longer avoid them."

They never called the police, for while they were still standing at the window they saw a car stop opposite the gate. A man got out, crossed the street, apparently unaware in his haste of the traffic from both sides, opened the gate and came running up to the house.

"It's that damn foreigner," said Mogens. At the same time Whitney recognized Severin.

They met him in the entrance. He still wore the raincoat but now its collar was turned down. His unshaven face looked sick with fatigue, his teeth more crooked than ever. Helge shied away from him, leaning against Whitney. "Watch out," she whispered. "Watch out, Whitney."

"Tried to reach you everywhere," said Severin, without the slightest attempt at politeness. "Frøken Rasmussen finally told me where I could find you." His voice was as impatient and arrogant as Whitney remembered it from their first meeting.

"I thought you'd gone," said Whitney. "Bag and all. Destination unknown. What are you doing here?"

"I just told you," said Severin, lighting a fresh cigarette at the stub of the old one. "Looking for you. Will you please stop interrupting me. I've found out where they are holding Anders."

"Where?"

Later they could never remember who asked the question.

"Ahrenshoop," said Severin. "A small seaside place, a fishing village on the German coast, Russian Zone, of course. That's where they're holding him—the German police—for the Russians."

"How did you find out?"

"I went to Gedser," said Severin. "As soon as you left, I took the train to Gedser."

"I didn't mean that," said Whitney sharply. "I meant from whom did you find out?"

"Connections."

"Only last night, early this morning rather, you told me you had no connections."

"In Copenhagen, no—in Gedser, yes. You didn't want to waste time going to Gedser, did you?"

"Who are they? Who told you?"

"Sorry," said Severin, "I can't give them away." Anger showed in his eyes. "Parker," he said, "why do you think I'm trying to break my neck? To amuse myself? I thought you might want to know so you wouldn't have to deliver the container."

Whitney took a deep breath. "Go over, you mean? Go over into the Russian Zone?"

"What else?" said Severin. "It's our only chance to try to save Anders. I know Ahrenshoop like my own pocket. I told you I lived in Ribnitz, just across the Bodden."

Whitney didn't answer. Severin's presence at this moment was ominous. Too well timed. Coming at a moment when all his hopes had broken down, when he was at a complete loss and, as their enemies must know, at a point of such despair that he would try the impossible. To send Severin with a message of where Anders was being held, to lure him, Whitney, into the lion's den, to make another attempt on his life, to play one man against the other, to get hold of the explosive without setting them free. . . .

"Who sent you this time?" he asked. "Dream-walking again? Delivering a message because you're too cowardly to kill yourself?"

"I came on my own," said Severin. "I don't care if I die or not. I told you, a man gets tired. I'm ready to come along with you, show you the way. . . ."

To make sure he would not leave Denmark, to deliver him personally to the people who at this moment might be holding his father.

"I don't think it can be done."

"Perhaps not," said Severin. "It won't be easy for there was no time to prepare anything. Still, police headquarters are at a formerly private villa outside Ahrenshoop proper. Not all of the beach is guarded.

There are spots the searchlights hardly reach. And the barometer is falling. We may have a chance."

"Don't go," said Helge suddenly, "don't go, Whit. It's a trap." She stopped abruptly as though aware only now that what she had said meant resigning herself to her brother's death.

Severin groped around in the deep bulging pockets of his raincoat. "I brought a map," he said, holding out a folded piece of paper. "The demarcation runs seven miles from the shore. We have to break through the German patrol boats."

Mogens had the face of a man hypnotized as Whitney unfolded the map and followed with his finger the pencil marks Severin had made. "We must be away well before dawn," Severin said. "We have to count that we'll need time with the kayaks even if we go as close as one mile to the shore."

"You've got it all figured out," said Mogens, "haven't you?" He turned to Whitney. "What do you say, Herre Parker?"

"It's your boat, Mogens."

"What are you talking about?" said Severin, apparently untouched by the general mistrust. "We can't take Mogens' boat." He laughed with impatient anger. "You'd need at least twelve hours to cover the distance between here and the German coast. Or do you want to land in broad daylight?"

Mogens nodded. "That's true," he said. "We would need at least twelve hours from here."

Severin shrugged. "As I said before, Parker, there's hardly any time. We have to use tonight or just forget about it."

Severin was right. They had only this night. Once dawn broke their last chance was gone. Staring at Severin, Whitney asked himself once more if his enemies, aware of the fact that he was ready to get in touch with the authorities, had sent him. At this moment they would not dare make a second attempt on his life in this country, but if they could lure him into their own camp . . . I must tell Ulla, he thought, to call the police, to tell them there is a dead man in this house, shot through the window. . . .

"What do you propose?" he asked.

"To go to Gedser," said Severin. "As quickly as we can. There's a man willing to take us across."

"But you just said you'd had no time to make preparations."

Severin smiled. "Only the most necessary ones," he said.

They were at sea, running before the wind.

The cutter they had found waiting for them in Gedser was a twenty-five-ton boat with a 50 h.p. Diesel motor. It had the measurements of the usual Danish fishing craft, a length of forty-five feet, a beam of four-teen and a half and a draught of a little more than eight. There were two masts rigged like a Bermudan ketch with mainsail, two jibs and one mizzen. Like Mogens' boat, it had a covered wheelhouse aft and a cabin with four bunks fore. And the man who owned it seemed as competent as Mogens but he was of small build, dark-skinned and silent. Whitney did not know what to make of him. He didn't speak a word to any of them but he seemed glad Mogens had come along to give a hand. The one deckhand, a young boy, looked like him, yet he seemed too young to have a son that age. Like him, the boy never spoke. The moment they had boarded the boat Severin seemed strangely in full command of everything.

"If the wind holds," he said, "we should make it in about two hours and a half. There's no point in your hanging around on deck, Parker. You'd better go and snatch some sleep." But Whitney had not been able to sleep.

He watched Helge, sitting opposite him. Dressed in slacks now and a turtleneck sweater, a stocking cap hiding her lovely hair, she looked more like a boy than a girl. And like a small boy who thinks it beneath him to show fear, her face betrayed nothing of what she was feeling.

"I should never have let you come."

She smiled at him. "Nothing could have stopped me." She held out her hand. "What good would life be to me without you?"

He shook his head. He could no longer understand why he had not insisted on her staying at the farm. But there had been no time for discussion. They had left immediately. With Severin, driving as if the devil were after them, they had made Gedser in just a little more than three hours. Only once, when the sun had set in an orange sky that changed rapidly to pale yellow, then reddened, had he exclaimed, "Thank God, that means rain and a dark night."

In Gedser Whitney had again tried to persuade Helge to stay behind, to wait for them in this Danish town on the furthermost point of Zealand. "Come on, come on," Severin had interrupted the discussion, "it's past ten already," and Helge had come. It was midnight now. The tension was almost unbearable.

Whitney could sit still no longer. He rose. "I'll just take a look outside."

It was dark. He almost tripped over the two kayaks which were lying over the closed hatch of the hold. That the boats had been there had raised another doubt in Whitney's mind. Everything seemed too well prepared when, as Severin had said, nothing had been prepared.

For the first sixteen miles they had made good time

with a fresh breeze from the northwest, but as Whitney came up to Mogens, he saw the fisherman trimming the mainsheet. "Wind slackening off," he said, and laughed, pointing at his sweater. "Haifisch I, we are. Shark's a fitting name for this, don't you think?" He laughed again, not laughter that was forced to ease his tension but the deep laughter of contentment. Bored with the peace, thought Whitney. A daredevil. Mogens was enjoying this.

Whitney entered the wheelhouse. Severin sat on the bunk reserved for the helmsman. Like Mogens, he was wearing a dark blue sweater with the German name of the boat. He had put a beret on his head which made him look like a wise, sad monkey.

" 'Box office' is the password," he was saying, "and don't dim your lights, whatever happens." He looked up, saw Whitney and frowned sharply in disapproval. "You should . . ." he said, and at this moment they were challenged. A Russian corvette lay ahead of them. And before anyone could say anything, Severin answered without hesitation, speaking in the foreign language as though it were his own.

The answer came. Whitney couldn't understand it, but Severin nodded in his direction. "We can pass," he said. He turned to the man at the wheel. "Proceed ahead to starboard, then dead ahead."

A chain of lights from the German patrol boats

fanned out to guard the German shore seven miles ahead of them, and only when, as ordered, they had moved through a gap between the boats, did Whitney dare speak.

"I didn't know you spoke Russian."

"Picked it up," said Severin. "Aren't you speaking Danish?"

For the first time since Whitney had met him, he saw the other man's eyes look gay, almost soft with happiness. Happiness that everything had gone better than he had hoped or happiness that Helge, Mogens and Whitney had followed him into the trap? Whatever it was, it was too late now to change anything. Then suddenly the silence was penetrated by a small steady sound. The sound of drops. It had begun to rain. Severin took a look at the glass. "Still falling," he said, with a sigh. He put his hand on Whitney's arm. "Time to get ready," he said, and to the man at the wheel, "If we're not back by four, four-thirty at the latest, go. It's up to you not to wait longer than is necessary to get home safely."

Twenty-five minutes later, with the mainsail lowered, the cutter was running slowly under headsails. When these were lowered, they dropped the anchor, snubbed the cable and let the boat swing in the tide. Here, so close to the shore, there was almost no wind and they had no difficulty lowering the dinghy with the three men and the two kayaks. Severin was the first to get away alone but Mogens nearly upset the second kayak, which was already manned by Whitney, as he climbed from the dinghy into the frail craft. Steadying it, Whitney stared through the darkness to where he supposed Helge was standing. They had not said good-bye, just looked at each other for a long moment and parted. Now he thought he could feel her presence above him. Oh my darling, he thought. Then they were away.

They had tied rags around the oars while still on board and they made no sound as Mogens and he, pad-dling quickly, followed Severin who had waited for them. The tide was with them. The rain fell more heav-ily now, drenching their heads and shoulders and arms while from the waist down their bodies were protected by the closed flaps. Behind them they could see the lights of the German patrol boats dancing on the quiet sea, far to their left the strong flashes of a lighthouse; ahead of them parts of a dark forest, of beach and dunes were lit at regular intervals by searchlights from watch-towers. But it was as Severin had said, there were dark pockets, and it was toward one of these that they headed.

Half an hour later there came to them, through the quiet and dark and rain, the voices of men. They stopped paddling, lowering themselves instinctively,

216

their bodies tense, their ears straining, their hearts pounding. "Two men patrol the coast every thousand yards," Severin had told them. A shout now from him and an answering rifle shot would alarm not only the village but the boats behind them. And the cutter would no more be able to get away than Mogens and he.

They could not see Severin, only hear his voice, incredibly close, almost inaudible the moment the guards had stopped talking. "Five minutes," he whispered, and in those five minutes they touched sand, shouldered their boats, ran across the beach and into the shelter of some low dunes. There they lay panting, listening for the guards to return, heard them come back, pass, go on. Severin tapped Whitney on the shoulder. At some time or other, on the boat, Severin had said that Mogens was to stay with the kayaks and wait while he and Whitney went on alone. Mogens had tried to argue, not wanting to be condemned to inactivity, but finally he had given in. Now, crouching between the dunes, then moving across a hard trodden path on his stomach, following the man ahead of him, Whitney felt easier for the first time. If Severin had wanted to betray them, he could have done so by now.

In front of him he heard Severin stop. Simultaneously he heard the sharp bark of a dog. The next moment he felt a cold nose nuzzling the back of his head, the warm

217

breath of the animal on his neck and, after he had been sniffed all over, heard the dog run off. They lay motionless, waiting, listening, then Severin moved on.

A few minutes later he rose. Before them loomed the dark shape of a house.

Whitney didn't hear the two light taps on the windowpane, he only heard the door being opened softly, a whisper, "Come in." A hand touched him, he was pulled into the house and it seemed an eternity until a light was turned on and he could see where he was.

He was standing in a small kitchen, its only window so carefully shaded as if the owners had been told to get ready for an air raid. A girl, rather young and surprisingly lovely, handed him a bottle of schnaps. But she didn't speak to him. She was addressing Severin. "You're late," she said. "You're quite terribly late."

Severin shrugged. "Did you get it? All I asked for?"

"I did. Wait here. I'll be back in a moment. I had to hide it. I didn't dare take it out before."

"I thought," said Whitney, sitting down on a kitchen stool and shaking his head at Severin as much as at himself, "that you had nothing prepared. The boat, the kayaks, now this, here . . ."

"Nothing is prepared," said Severin, taking another swallow from the bottle, "nothing, that is, which concerns Anders. This here . . ." and he made one of his vague, impatient gestures. "I have been planning my

218

father's escape ever since I got away. That's why I kept in contact with people here and know about the man who owns the cutter. . . ."

Whitney understood suddenly the reason for the poverty of Severin's room in Copenhagen. Otto Severin had saved his money to make freedom possible for his old father. He was not only risking a dream, a goal he had set for himself, but his life and that of his father, to help Anders Ørsted.

Perhaps because Whitney colored deeply, Severin guessed what he had thought. "You didn't believe me," he said. "Well, I must say that for a man who didn't trust me, you showed quite a bit of courage."

"I thought . . ." Whitney shook his head. "First I suspected Mogens, then you, then Gabel and finally, when it turned out that Larsen was the brain behind all this, and you appeared just when my offer to exchange him for Anders had been turned down by their murdering Larsen . . ."

"Larsen?" Severin stared at Whitney in disbelief. "Larsen?"

His lips opened, closed and opened again, but in the end he said nothing. And what was there to say? One could only wonder at human nature, wonder if one would ever dare rely again on one's own judgment and instinct, wonder if a shock like this would ever pass or keep burning like a sore in one's mind and heart. For a moment the two men, sitting in the quiet, dimly lit kitchen, waiting for the girl to reappear, forgot the danger surrounding them; then Whitney, watching Severin's dark sad face, found himself saying, "Anders would not have wanted you to do this."

"I might never have had the courage," Severin answered, "if you had not doubted me. I could not bear the thought that Anders might suspect me, too. I had to prove to him . . ." He lifted the bottle, tipped it back, swallowed and sighed. "I had to prove something to myself. You see, when I panicked last night, when I didn't have the guts to go to the police or to tell Helge the truth, I could not forgive myself. I lay awake thinking while you slept. If you bow to terror, you play their game. Once you allow anyone to terrorize you, you will be terrorized all your life. Terror corrupts. Pretty soon you'll be terrorizing others. Then I made my choice. Life doesn't mean anything if you can't rid yourself of fear."

And Whitney understood that in a way Severin was now committing the suicide he had planned.

Then, with the danger gone that Severin might be luring them into a trap from which they could not escape, his mind returned to the danger facing them. "What about Anders? Have you any plans?"

"Yes," said Severin. Just then the door opened and the girl came in carrying a bundle. She put it on the table for Severin to open. To his amazement Whitney saw two Russian uniforms, a major's and a sergeant's.

A faint smile lighted up his eyes. The moment of surprise, he thought, remembering in a flash all sorts of examples in history in which confusion had been the decisive factor. Only in the last war, the Germans had taken one of the strongest fortresses in Belgium because they had appeared dressed in Dutch uniforms.

"The moment of surprise," said Severin. "It is all we have. And I was not even sure she could procure them."

He nodded at the girl who withdrew. Whitney looked after her. "How does it work?"

Severin stripped. "Code," he answered. "I phoned this morning. Each letter stands for something. Until now it has not been discovered. I hope . . ." He fingered the pockets of the blouse and nodded to himself as he pulled out an envelope and stuck it back in again. "I'll have to ask you not to speak, not a word, whatever happens."

"Of course not."

He looked at the frail dark man dressed as a Russian major. Would he be able to go through with his part? Whitney had seen him break down in his room only last night, now he was putting their lives into the hands of a man he knew could lose his nerve.

"Severin," he said, remembering the first rule of those who had served in the underground, "we must not use our guns. Under no circumstances must a shot be fired. If we have to . . ." He pointed at the two daggers. "But no shot. It would alarm them all."

They left as they had entered, through the back door, but this time they took a path running behind a row of houses. From here they no longer could see the sea, only smell it. It was still raining, raining more heavily than when they had landed. Every few paces they withdrew into the shelter of the houses, listening for steps from the main road that ran parallel with the path. Avoiding the Vopo, the People's Police Patrol, timing their steps to fit into the minutes when the Vopo had passed, they finally dared cross the main road.

The village lay behind them; to their left was the beach, to their right, between patches of fir, were the small hills formed by the dunes on which a few single houses stood. They moved between these until, quite suddenly, the land was flat and they could see ahead of them the building which was now the police station.

Once it had been a private villa, erected by General Hoffman, the victor of Tannenberg, during the First World War, as a place where he might take a few days' rest. Its upper floor lay in darkness; only in one room downstairs were lights burning. Approaching it from the back, they had to pass an apparently newly built small barrack. They had hardly got by that when, to his surprise, Whitney saw that Severin had dropped all caution. He walked erect, no longer caring apparently who might hear their steps or see them. They came into the circle of light over the entrance door. For just one second then Severin stood motionless, the next moment he was hammering on the door with the butt of his revolver.

Through the lighted, iron-barred windows, Whitney saw a guard jump to attention, a blond young man nudging a second one who had fallen asleep in his chair. He was a little older and his hair was dark. Severin was shouting, shouting in Russian.

The door flew open. They stepped in, Severin still speaking Russian, angrily, noisily.

The two guards on duty, obviously surprised, unable to understand a word, tried to speak, to ask a question, but Severin waved them aside, addressing them in German now, broken German with a heavy accent. "Where is your captain? Damn it, where is he? Why isn't he here?"

"Sir," said the one who looked older, "Captain Muller is asleep. It is night."

"Wake him," yelled Severin, and while the blond one rushed up a staircase, swinging into what must formerly have been the entrance hall, Severin turned to the dark one. "The prisoner," he said. "Ørsted. Bring him in."

"Impossible, sir. Orders are . . ."

Severin began to shout in Russian again. Whitney, as bidden, said not a word. He stood near the door, at a respectful distance from his major, telling himself it couldn't work, that any moment now Severin's nerves would break, that he would make a mistake, that he might be able to fool two young guards but never an older and experienced policeman.

Steps were sounding on the floor above him, the blond guard came running down the stairs, standing at attention even before a middle-aged gray-haired man, buckling his belt, appeared at the head of the stairs.

"Hurry up, Captain," Severin told him angrily, "I haven't got all night. What kind of setup is this anyway? I'll report you for laziness, for slackness, for . . ."

Captain Muller was saluting. His eyes were heavy with sleep but a vein at his temple was hammering. He was, Whitney saw, not only surprised but afraid.

Severin, apparently, saw it, too. "Your name?" he yelled. "Age? Where were you born? Since when are you in command of this station?" He turned to Whitney, speaking in Russian, then addressed one of the guards. "Give my man pen and paper."

Watching Severin in stunned admiration, Whitney again had the feeling that at one point or another Severin had left the world of the living. Such superb negation of all the dangers of discovery was not quite

224

human. And then he knew that Severin could act as he did only because nothing at this moment mattered to him. Neither his own life nor that of those involved. Compared to Severin, the captain, the two guards and Whitney himself seemed like figures moved by a robot. He stared at Severin and because he was impressed himself he understood the power the other was able to exercise over the three Germans. Still he could not believe that the spell would last.

"Sir," said the captain, "if the major would be kind enough to . . ."

Severin did not let him finish. "Ørsted," he said. "How long am I to wait for him? Do you think my colonel wants to sit up all night waiting to question him?"

"Question?" repeated the captain. "But he has been questioned already."

"Not by Colonel Mansky," said Severin. "I've got to get him to Ribnitz."

"I have no orders. . . ."

"Orders?" said Severin, and reached into the pocket of his blouse. "There are your orders."

He threw the envelope onto the table. Whitney, pretending to scribble something on the pad he had been handed, could see that the paper the captain was unfolding was stamped all over and written in Russian lettering. The German stared at it. Unable to understand it, he seemed not to know what to do, admit that he could not read the language or pretend he could. He was frowning with concentration and Whitney suddenly had the impression that the man was weighing the situation from the point of view of a man who had never seen a Russian, only heard about them, the rumors of a frightened people, of tortures in the night, of their cruelty, their complete unpredictability. Perhaps, too, that this little coastal village, just across the Bodden from Ribnitz, had not yet suffered too much under Russian rule and that the captain was picturing in his mind the consequences his behavior might have upon the whole community.

Severin hammered with his fists on the table, so suddenly, so noisily, that the captain almost dropped the envelope. He looked up, looked at the angry face of Severin, then nodded slowly.

There was a moment when Whitney felt the sweat pouring down his spine, the moment when the guard disappeared through a door to the left of the staircase until the door opened again. Anders Ørsted entered the guard room, as tall as Whitney remembered him, carrying himself erect, his shoulders unbent as though nothing, neither the idea of torture or death, could destroy his dignity. But his broad open face looked pale, a three days' growth of beard made his chin look less strong, his whitish blond hair had lost its silvery shine and fell unkempt over his high, square forehead. And he blinked like a man whose eyes could not get used to the brightness of light.

Whitney stared at those large gray eyes and as he stared, he saw the deadness go out of them. Stark naked fear showed in them as they recognized slowly, unbelievingly, the two men in their Russian uniforms. His mouth began to tremble, his lips opened, closed, without having uttered a sound. He moved a step back, as though trying to withdraw voluntarily to his cell, as though he wanted to tell them to go, now, when there was still perhaps time. But the guard who had fetched him pushed him roughly forward. And Whitney realized with immense surprise that the fear Ørsted showed, the fear for their lives, which was endangering them all, was taken by the captain as fear of the Russians.

He never knew if it was Anders' horror that moved the policeman to pity or if, at this moment, when he was handing over his prisoner, some sense of his own authority returned to him. "Sir," he said, "I have to ask you to wait. It will take only a few minutes but I would like to telephone Ribnitz for confirmation of your . . ."

Severin turned on him. "What," he yelled, pointing at Ørsted, "no handcuffs? You dare to let an enemy of the people run around without handcuffs?"

The captain swallowed so hard, his Adam's apple

showed over his collar. "Handcuffs," he said, and the blond young guard pulled open a desk, took out a pair of handcuffs and walked up to Anders who held out his hands.

"I assure you, sir," Captain Muller was stammering, "there was no need of handcuffs. We . . ."

"An enemy of the people," repeated Severin, snatching up the keys. "You'll be on trial for this." He swung around, marched to the door, Anders fell in behind him, Whitney brought up the rear.

Then they were outside, marching down the main road, marching as long as they could be seen from the police station, their steps sounding through the night. Somehow Whitney could not believe it. The moment of surprise, he thought again, the moment of confusion. It explained why the most carefully worked out plans could fail and sheer luck make the impossible possible. Men, after all, were not machines. Their fears might make criminals of them or martyrs, cowards or heroes, each responding and reacting according to the powers of his imagination and nerves.

They reached complete darkness and Severin, unlocking Anders' handcuffs, said under his breath, "Cut across the beach. Keep to the left and run for it, but take off your boots first."

Like ghosts they disappeared, none knowing where the others were, running, stopping, crouching, each on his own. Then through the night came the ugly sound of a gull screeching, stopped, came again. Mogens, thought Whitney.

He was the first to reach the fisherman. He threw himself down on the cold wet sand between the cluster of dunes. To his utter horror he could see Mogens. He looked up into the sky. The faintest gray of dawn was creeping across the horizon. A few seconds later there was a tiny sound. Moving on his stomach, Anders joined them and a minute later Severin's body stirred in the grass of the dunes. None of them spoke but their hands were trembling. Then Mogens whispered, "The patrol passes every five minutes. We can't get across the beach and into the boats and more than twenty yards away in that time. They'll see us and shoot. With dawn breaking we need at least ten minutes to get out of sight. They . . ." He broke off. Close to them they could hear the voices of two men talking, complaining about the rain. Then the voices faded and Mogens spoke again.

"The next time they come, we'll have to do something about them." Their faces were so close they could feel each others' breath. "You and Anders take the boats and get to the water as soon as we've lured them away from the beach," said Whitney. "Severin and I, in our uniforms, have a better chance to surprise them."

He and Severin moved a distance of about twenty

feet away to a point where the dunes formed another small, deep gap. There they hid in the tough grass. They didn't have to wait long until they heard once more the sound of voices. Whitney lifted his head. They were sturdy young men. He put two fingers between his lips and made a strange sucking noise which could have been human but which also might have been an animal. The guards stopped, looked around. "Heard something, Karl?"

"Sure did. Can't figure out what it was."

"Think we should have a look?"

"Came from behind the dunes."

Whitney could see them turn. They were coming in his direction, uncocking their rifles. "Get their rifles," he whispered. "Don't let them fire. The rifles first."

They lay motionless and the steps drew closer, mounting the elevation of the dune.

They jumped at the same time. They jumped from the ground like fish out of water, jumped at the rifles and knocked them out of the hands of the surprised men before they had a chance to lift them and aim. The next second they were a knot of four fighting, straining bodies.

How long their fight lasted, Whitney did not know. He had bound and gagged his man and dragged him out of sight before he was even aware that Severin had been less lucky. Severin was lying on top of the man he had attacked, both hands around the guard's neck, trying to keep him from shouting, while the man was stabbing at Severin's back with a dagger.

A strange and terrible anger seized Whitney and he struck blindly at the German, hitting him again and again, even after the man had dropped the knife and was offering no more resistance.

It was Severin who stopped him. "Don't lose any more time," he whispered. He was lying a few feet away and around him the sand was no longer gray—it was red.

For a moment Whitney stood motionless. Then he bent. "You'll make it," he said. "You'll make it all right." And as though his words were convincing, Severin tried to get up.

Half carrying, half leading him, Whitney reached Mogens and Anders at the water line. They were in the kayaks and away, paddling rapidly until, after fifty yards, they could no longer see the shore and knew they could not be seen either through the fog and rain.

If Severin dies, Whitney thought, I'll never forgive myself. He acted as he did only because I . . . He was at the end of his strength, he should have stayed with Anders. I should have taken Mogens to attack the guard. But he knew he hadn't done so because Anders might have needed help.

"Parker," said Severin.

Whitney could not see the face of the mortally wounded man behind him, only hear his whisper. "I was wrong a little while ago when I told you once you are rid of fear you are free. You are free only when you care for nobody in the world. But if you stop caring, life isn't worth living."

The rain fell, the fog swayed like a gray curtain in the early morning wind. Suddenly, unexpectedly, the cutter loomed up, dead ahead of them. At 4:40, with the wind abaft the beam, they slipped through the German patrol boats without being challenged.

They were in the cabin, Severin, bandaged, lying on the bunk, the others sitting across from him, close together, watching him. "I'm all right," Severin whispered. "Go on, Anders." His whisper carried a strange urgency as though he realized his time was running out and he didn't want to die before he knew exactly what had happened.

"There's nothing much to tell," said Anders. "I always trusted you, Otto. That I didn't mention the container or Whitney's coming was merely because I did not want you to get involved should anything happen. Your situation as a refugee from the East Zone was precarious enough. But of course I told Larsen and Gabel, told them because I thought they might be of help in case something went wrong."

232

He paused, closing his eyes for a moment, and with his eyes closed his face looked incredibly sad. "I couldn't sleep the night after Mogens brought me the container. That I couldn't analyze the stuff kept me awake. I thought I'd have another try before cabling Whitney but when I crossed the meadow I saw somebody run out of the lab. There was moonlight, yet I could not make out who it was nor could I catch up with him. It might have been an ordinary burglar but what would anybody want to steal from a laboratory? Yet when I entered I found that it had been thoroughly searched. And of course I could only think that somebody must have heard of Mogens' catch. That's why I didn't call in the police but decided to find out myself if anybody was after the explosive."

Anders sighed. The lines around his full, generous mouth seemed deeper than Whitney remembered, like finely imbedded scars. "I knew about the Frigga being empty and rented it the morning after the burglary. From then on, instead of going to my office or working in the lab on the farm, I went to Viken every day. Whoever followed me to the Frigga could be interested only in the explosive."

His voice was almost inaudible for a moment, as though he did not want to speak about it. "I didn't think at the time that the traitor might be one of my closest friends, rather that one of them might have mentioned it carelessly."

His voice rose. He was speaking impersonally now. "On the second day I knew the Frigga had been searched for I found some of my things not as I had left them, but of course I had no idea by whom or on whose orders. I did notice a man hanging around whom I suspected of watching me. So I decided to set a trap. I chose the morning Whit was arriving, to make it look as if I had gone to Viken to fetch the container and take it to the Holger Works. That morning I pretended to dig up something in the dunes. Then I went back to the house and waited. I didn't have to wait long. When I looked out of the window a few minutes later I saw a man I'd never seen before, right in front of the house. When I went to the other side, there was the man who had been watching me all along. I realized then how dangerous my situation was."

Just as I imagined it, thought Whitney, and he remembered the moment before Mogens' blow had hit him so unexpectedly, how he had stood at the window trying to picture Anders standing there. Now Anders was looking at him, his eyes, his smile expressing better than words his deep gratification that Whitney had understood his own motives so precisely.

"I had drawn the map and written the note and mailed it before I entered the Frigga that morning, just in case something like this should happen, though I must confess I never thought I would be kidnapped. I thought I was going to discover who was after the explosive through the man who fell for my ruse. I went to my boat then, and they followed me in theirs. It was on the sea that they took me. I was helpless because they had drained the gasoline from my tank."

"Did they hurt you?" Helge laid a hand on her brother's arm.

Anders smiled at her. "They questioned me, that whole Friday and that whole night. Germans. Until Saturday afternoon. Then they stopped. Whit had arrived and they knew he knew, and of course Larsen thought you could persuade him to surrender the container in exchange for me. Later they tried to make me sign a note they had composed. I refused and finally they were satisfied with what I wrote.

"I don't know what to say to either of you—to Whit, that he found out what I failed to discover, who was working for the Russians, and for understanding, for protecting the explosive. To you, Otto, for . . ."

"Don't thank me," said Severin. "Unlike Whitney, my motives were completely egoistic, endangering all of them—Helge and Parker and Mogens. If we had not been so lucky . . . so lucky . . ." he repeated, "lucky . . ."

They left the cabin then, Helge and Whitney and Mogens, leaving Anders and Otto Severin alone.

Now it was quite light. Whitney put his arm around Helge's shoulders. In two hours or so they would be back in Denmark.

There are moments in life when nothing seems real, neither past nor present, and this was such a moment. Nothing of what had happened from the second when he had first read the notice of Anders Ørsted's death in the paper nor the events between that Friday and this Monday morning seemed in any way possible or true. Yet they were. But Whitney only realized it when Helge turned in his arms, staring back in the direction of the German coast, then turned again and, looking ahead, said in a small, amazed voice, "I didn't think, Whit, that there was a future left for us—a future we could share."

About the Author

Citizen of the world, Miss Albrand spent much of her early life in Europe—France, Germany, Switzerland, Italy and Holland—before settling down to a 106-acre farm in New Jersey. At the outbreak of the last war she had a home in London and a villa in Italy. The home was bombed and the villa confiscated, but Miss Albrand fortunately was safe in America, which is actually her native land. Her great-grandfather renounced his Polish title to become a missionary among the Indians and her grandmother was the first white child to be born in the Chippewa settlement.

Though born in Rostock, Germany, and educated on the continent, Miss Albrand's first real home was with a London aunt. After a succession of jobs as secretary and reporter, she began her distinguished career as a novelist. Out of her cosmopolitan background she has created eleven novels, eight of them stories of adventure and suspense, dealing with the settings she knows so well and emphasizing the varied mentalities of the peoples she has met.

In private life she is Mrs. Joseph Lowengard and divides her time between New York and Pattenburg, New Jersey. She is devoted to her farm, gardening, book-collecting and dogs, especially skye terriers. She also manages to continue her travels—in recent years to the Near East and Scandinavia—to absorb fresh material for her books, a number of which have appeared in magazine serials and in the movies.